THE OFFER

THE DEADLY DECISIONS COLLECTION

D.L. WOOD

SILVERGLASS
PRESS

THE OFFER
The Deadly Decisions Collection
Copyright ©2023 by D.L. Wood
All rights reserved.

THE OFFER is a work of fiction. Names, characters, places and incidents either are the product of the author's imagination or are used fictitiously. Any resemblance to actual persons, living or dead, events or locales is entirely coincidental and beyond the intent of either the author or publisher.

No part of this book may be reproduced or transmitted in any form or by any means, electronic or mechanical, including photocopying, recording, or by any information storage and retrieval system, without the written permission of the author, except where permitted by law.

First edition
Print Version ISBN 9798851958250
Silverglass Press

D.L. Wood
www.dlwoodonline.com
Huntsville, Alabama

*To Judy Wallis, the best mother-in-law a girl could ask for.
I love you with all my heart.*

1

ADDIE

"Aaa-deee-laaide?"

The haunting, sing-song voice pierced Addie's hiding place, sending chills like spiders across her skin. She had crawled in and closed the door behind her, praying she wouldn't be found. Now, propelled by the voice hunting her, she attempted to shrink back further into the tiny space. As she had barely fit inside to start with, she only managed to contract into a tighter ball.

She squeezed her eyes shut, one thought echoing in her mind as if thinking it would make it true.

Don't find me.

Don't find me.

Thunder boomed and Addie flinched as the heavens roared, dumping a deluge of angry rain onto the Victorian mansion's roof. Over the din, the sound of her name, each syllable dripping with malice, cut through to where she was concealed on the topmost floor.

"Aaa-deee-laaide? Are you ignoring me?"

Addie angled her head and strained to listen. Where was the voice coming from? How close was her pursuer?

"Are you pretending you can't hear me?" The words were sharp-nailed claws, brutally scraping Addie's gut and stripping away her courage. She bit her lip to keep herself from crying out in desperation. Were they on the same floor? In the same room? She couldn't answer either question, which meant she had no idea how long she had left.

Before I'm found.

Before I die.

Addie sucked in a quiet breath as a jolt of electric terror shot through her.

Calm down. You have to calm down.

She had to control her runaway panic. She needed to be ready. Because she was alone.

Alone with a killer.

Fervent, desperate prayers issued from the deepest part of her soul, begging God for protection, for rescue.

"You can't hiiiii-de from me. Not forrr-ehh-ver, Adelaide!"

Did the voice sound a bit...muffled? Hope flickered in Addie's chest.

Is it coming from farther away than before? Maybe there's a chance—

Hope died as a yell rang out, loud, annoyed, and unquestionably nearer, removing any doubt the distance between Addie and death was closing.

"I'll find you eventually! I will!"

No, no, no...

Time was running out. Her time. Her life.

"You should have taken your chances outside. At least you'd

have given yourself a shot." The torrential rain and the killer's voice invaded Addie's brain, bashing into one another like battling waves, churning her fear, hurling her pounding heart against her ribs.

"The storm would have made it harder to catch you! This house might be big, but there are only so many rooms to hide in!"

For several moments, no more words came, but the silence that followed was equally chilling. Addie held her breath, sweat trickling down her brow, and her body shaking as she waited for the worst to come. She clasped her right hand with her left, trying to still them.

"Come ooouu-t, come ooouu-t, wherever you are. Aaa-deee-laaide…"

She had nowhere to go. It was like hiding in her own coffin.

Once the killer reached her, that was exactly what it would be.

2

ADDIE
DAYS EARLIER

"Did you see those plates, Chef?"

Addie wiped her hands on her apron, feeling a grin split her face. She turned to see Gillian mirroring her smile, a rare occurrence for the high-strung manager of East to West. Addie's American fusion restaurant in Greenwich Village had been open for six months and the fact that it was finally filling the dinner service was cause enough for celebration. But this evening something even better had happened.

"He cleaned them," Gillian said, a gleam in her eyes. "That's plural—as in, all of them."

Addie nodded. "I saw Derek bring them back. It's a good sign."

Tonight they managed to satisfy the impossibly atmospheric standards of Jonas Carter, one of the toughest restaurant critics in Manhattan. Not that he complimented them, or said anything resembling a favorable opinion about the food or service, but critics rarely finished everything on their plates. Gillian was right, that *was* a good sign. It likely meant a glowing review was on the way. The kind of press that would ensure the status of East to West as a "must visit" in the neighborhood and secure its viability—and Addie's financial stability—for the foreseeable future.

Thank goodness, because her finances had been iffy for a while now. Opening a restaurant in Manhattan was all-consuming and expensive. Addie had taken out loans and used the inheritance her grandparents had left her to get the place up and running. Six months in and that money was nearly gone. She had tried to make it last by doing whatever she could to strip down her expenses—keeping the lights and air conditioning off in her apartment, eating lots of cereal, and so on. Addie also let more than a few personal bills go unpaid and satisfied the restaurant's creditors instead. When she couldn't keep on without a cash infusion, Addie ended up getting a loan from her parents. Her pride had taken a serious hit.

Now maybe things would turn around. Then she would repay her parents and start standing on her own two feet.

My own two feet.

The thought warmed her. She had put everything into this business. Not just her money, but all of herself. Her time, her energy, her passion. Every waking hour. She gave up all the other things she loved to do—hanging out with friends, going to the gym, reading with kids in the after-school program—because pursuing this dream didn't allow for anything but the dream. At least not right now. One day she would be able to pick those things back up.

Maybe that day is closer than it was yesterday.

Clanking, banging, and the upbeat jabber of the staff resounded through the space, bouncing off the stainless steel that was everywhere, drawing Addie out of her thoughts. They might have locked the front door behind the last guest twenty minutes earlier, but the kitchen was still alive, in the full throes of post-dinner cleanup.

The clamor fed Addie's soul. She loved the atmosphere. She loved the people. She might be tired by the time this part rolled around, but there was always joy in it. Tonight that was doubly true after the food critic's positive reaction, giving her a much-needed boost as she entered the twelfth hour of her shift. Sadly, it did nothing to dampen the ache in her knees. Standing that long tended to take its toll, even on a twenty-nine-year-old.

"Chef?" one of the busboys called from behind her. Addie turned to see Marcus, an early-twenties Broadway hopeful sticking his head through the swinging door into the dining room. "A woman's out front, begging to see you."

Addie's brow furrowed. She occasionally met with suppliers after closing, but wasn't expecting anyone this evening. Besides, they would have used the rear entrance. "Who is it?"

Marcus shrugged. "Some Uptown hoity-toit by the looks of her. Got a car and driver too. I told her we were closed but she said it's urgent."

"Sounds persistent."

"Well, she's barking at me through the glass so...yeah."

Addie's lips pressed together in amused curiosity. "Okaaaay." She slipped off her apron and hung it on her reserved hook. "Bark back that I'm coming."

Marcus disappeared and Addie took a quick look in the small mirror hanging on the wall by the door. *Not horrible,* she appraised, *but not fantastic either.* Strands of her long, straight sable tresses had escaped from her tight bun. She smoothed them against her scalp, tucking them back in as best she could and rubbing away the mascara smudges under her eyes. Little remained of the rest of her minimal makeup, worn away over the hours by constant heat in the kitchen and the ever-present slight perspiration it produced. Even her dark brown irises seemed cloudy, the whites of her eyes a little bloodshot.

What had she expected? It was the end of the shift, half an hour into the next day for goodness' sake.

Oh well.

Resigning herself to being the disheveled mess that was the badge of a working chef, Addie pushed through the swinging door into a short hallway leading into the dining room. The contemporary-appointed space was relatively small, but she had made the most of it by packing tables into every square inch, like the majority of Manhattan restaurants. Through the legs of the chairs already flipped upside down on the tabletops, she saw a woman on the sidewalk on the other side of the glass-paneled front door.

As soon as Addie unlocked it, the woman charged through as if taking refuge from someone in hot pursuit. She turned, straightened to her full height, and—after adjusting the designer purse on her arm that cost more than Addie made in a month—locked eyes with her.

"You're the chef? Adelaide Nichols?" she asked, plastering on a too-brilliant smile. On four-inch heels, she towered over Addie's five-foot-three frame, though her volumized blond hair was partially responsible for at least a couple of those inches. It fell to her collarbone, a single length of loose waves that was striking against her black silk shirt.

"Chef and owner," Addie answered. "And you are?"

The woman held out a hand adorned with so much chunky gold jewelry it likely required weight training to lift it. "Monica. Monica Farrow."

The gesture was awkwardly formal, but Addie shook her hand anyway, feeling a bit silly. Going by the faint veins in her hands, Addie guessed Ms. Farrow was in her early forties. She also suspected—given the complete lack of facial wrinkles—the woman was working very hard to hold on to her thirties, no matter how long ago they had passed.

"What can I do for you, Ms. Farrow? We're closed, but my employee said it was urgent."

"Yes. Yes, it is. And it's Monica, please." She exhaled, dropping her shoulders. "I have a bit of a problem and you may be the only one who can help."

"How's that?"

"Well"—she sighed again before diving in—"it's my husband's fiftieth birthday. He didn't want to make a huge thing of it. He's quite private. Doesn't care for a lot of people or a lot of fuss, but he loves our little vacation home. So when I suggested a simple, long weekend there, he utterly loved the idea."

She paused, eyeing Addie as if waiting for a response, though Addie didn't have the slightest notion what she expected from her.

Addie tilted her head. "I'm sorry. I still don't see how I can help."

Mrs. Farrow splayed her hands in front of herself. "I hired a private chef to come. We've done it before and it's wonderful. I was going to have Louis cook all of Richard's favorites...but, well...we've just had a falling out. I don't understand what went wrong. Something about me not 'paying him enough to be *that* particular about what I wanted, and why wasn't I letting him handle it,' and...he *bailed* on me. *Two hours ago!*" Mrs. Farrow's eyes went wide, her frustration evident. "Can you believe it? Said he wasn't coming and told me to make other arrangements. *The night before we leave.* I mean, how unprofessional can a person be?"

Mrs. Farrow shifted her weight to the other high heel. "It's Thursday night, it's late, and I'm thinking, 'How am I supposed to find someone at this hour? This will ruin everything.' Especially because his kids aren't going to be there—"

"Mrs. Farrow—"

"Monica."

The Offer

"Okay—Monica. I'm sorry, but if you're suggesting I take your chef's place, starting tomorrow morning, I can't do it. I can't step away from the restaurant—"

Monica held up a hand. "Before you say no, hear me out. As I was panicking at home trying to think of who to call, I suddenly remembered Richard ate here a couple of times recently and mentioned how much he enjoyed it. He fell in love with your dessert. Some kind of caramel and coffee thing—"

Addie nodded, knowing precisely the dessert she was talking about. One of her signature items. "The sea-salt-caramel-coffee mousse with dark chocolate shavings?" The embellished description tumbled out, making her sound pretentious, and she fought the urge to cringe at herself.

Monica didn't seem to care, her eyes brightening. She pointed a bejeweled finger at Addie. "Yes, yes! That's it! He said it was divine and when I remembered, I thought"—she grasped Addie's hand like a castaway clinging to a life preserver—"you could be my salvation. Please don't let Richard's fiftieth fall apart. It's the only gift I planned on giving him. Please. I'm begging you."

It wasn't hard to see that the woman was desperate. She was flashing doe-eyes suggesting that a "no" from Addie would result in a river of tears. But something was inherently off-putting about her. Addie couldn't pinpoint the problem—maybe the entitled air about the woman, or the disingenuous vibe she gave off. Whatever it was, it made the thought of working for her in any capacity unappealing.

Still, Addie was sympathetic. Having your well-laid plans for a loved one's big birthday fall apart was awful. Of course, in this case, the plans falling apart meant some rich person wouldn't have a private chef preparing upscale cuisine in their vacation home for the weekend. Not exactly an end-of-the-world situation. Certainly not enough of a sob story to convince Addie to leave the restaurant for four whole days. "I wish I could help, but there's no way—"

"Ten thousand dollars," Monica interrupted, her features turning to granite in instantaneous seriousness, a look that didn't fit the personality she had presented thus far.

A flush of heat rolled through Addie.

Did I hear her right?

"Did you say—"

"Ten thousand dollars for one long weekend. Four days. It's what I was going to pay Louis."

"Are you serious?" Addie said, the outrageous number causing her brain to buzz. "Ten thousand dollars for four days?"

Monica cocked her head, one of her eyebrows rising. "Well, yes, Ms. Nichols...or sorry, *Chef* Nichols. I'm more than happy to pay well for excellent service. After Richard's compliments, I know you're worth it. He's very critical, so if you have him singing your praises, you must be good. Plus, I understand this is inconvenient for you, with it being such short notice and having to leave tomorrow morning, so I've thrown in a little bonus."

Monica laid a pleading hand on Addie's forearm. "Say you'll come. I don't know what I'll do if you don't." She continued as if Addie already said yes, pulling a manilla envelope from her bag. "I have a couple of references here if you need them. They'll vouch for me. Since it's too late tonight to reach out to them, you won't be able to talk to them beforehand. But you can call them on the way and if you don't like what they say, the driver will turn right around and bring you back. You won't want to, though. I promise this will be the easiest money you ever make. And..." She paused, narrowing her eyes conspiratorially. "...having someone who runs in our circles indebted to your restaurant isn't the worst thing. We can throw a lot of business your way."

Ten thousand dollars. For four days.

"Inside the envelope is a list of what Louis had us stock already. You can text me anything else you need. Or bring it from your kitchen supplies if that's more convenient. We'll reimburse you, of course."

It was too unbelievable to comprehend. All the things that amount of money could do, the problems it would solve, spun through Addie's mind. She had been praying for a solution to her financial difficulties and waiting—and waiting—on God to provide. Now, here this woman was, right in front of her, offering an answer. It wasn't a permanent fix, but could be a temporary one. All it required was four days.

I can manage four days.

Gillian would be at the restaurant to deal with the management side of things and her sous chef could take over the kitchen. He needed a test drive anyway. One day she would be out sick, or—in her dreams—on a vacation, and he would have to be able to run the place on his own. This weekend would be as good a time as any. He wouldn't care about the short notice. He had been hinting at wanting a chance to prove himself.

"Ten thousand dollars?" Addie asked, hearing the doubt in her own voice.

One corner of Monica's mouth slid up. "Ten thousand."

Addie couldn't believe it. First the bookings. Then the critic. Now, ten grand dropping into her lap?

Weird vibe or not, it's too good to turn down.

Addie shrugged. "Well...yeah, okay. If you're serious. I guess you've got yourself a chef."

"Wonderful!" Monica said, breaking into a grin and holding the envelope out to Addie. "All my information is in here along with five thousand cash." Addie took it, her heart doing a little flip. She had never held that much money in her hands. "I'll give you the other half afterward. Text me your address and a driver will swing by to pick you up at six."

Addie's nose scrunched in distaste at the thought of having to be ready so early. She wasn't typically out of bed until after ten.

"I know it's early," Monica said, offering up a pitying smile that didn't seem at all heartfelt, "but it's a bit of a drive. You can nap on the way if you need to."

Addie calculated that if she gathered supplies from the kitchen, left within the hour, got home and packed, she might manage a few hours of sleep before six. She nodded. "Okay. Six it is."

Monica silently clapped her hands together as she let out a throaty squeal. "Richard's going to love this. It'll be the perfect surprise. He's such a foodie." She spun on her Jimmy Choos and strode to the entrance. "I'll see you around one in the afternoon," she called jauntily, holding up a slender hand and wiggling her fingers.

"Wait, um, Monica?"

Monica halted, her hand clutching the doorknob, swiveling to meet Addie's gaze over one shoulder. "Yes?"

"You never said where we're going?"

Monica pursed her lips and her forehead attempted to wrinkle, though it largely lost the battle to however many syringes of Botox resided there. "Didn't I?" Monica waved the question off. "It's on the sheet along with all the other instructions," she said, then waltzed out, offering a casual, "See you tomorrow!" without looking in Addie's direction.

As the door clicked behind Monica, Addie undid the envelope's metal clasp and extracted a thin stack of papers. The top one spelled out all the basic information she would need, including the house address.

Number One, Spirits Island, New York.

3

NOT ADDIE

It's happening.

Up to this point, doubts existed about the plan. Doubts about whether it would ever kick off. Doubts about whether, once it did, it would succeed. But things had started rolling and, so far, it seemed to be working.

For now, there was also still wiggle room. The opportunity to turn back, to stop, if it became too risky. Though, pretty soon it would be too late to unbake the cake.

Don't kid yourself. Deep down, you know that no matter how risky the situation becomes, you won't stop. Because there is no alternative. And there isn't any more time. That's the one thing you know for certain.

Something else existed alongside that sense of certainty but evaded a label. It took some concentration, but in the end, recognition gelled, birthing a wicked grin.

Anticipation.

The name of that something was anticipation.

The anticipation of everybody getting exactly what they deserve.

4

ADDIE

Addie barely managed four hours of sleep before trudging into the elevator of her third-story Brooklyn apartment, handing off her luggage to the driver of the black Mercedes-Benz that showed up for her, and crawling into its backseat. Despite the bumps and turns as they made their way out of Manhattan, she soon fell asleep, waking three-and-a-half hours later to find they were well out of the city, already halfway to the Thousand Islands archipelago that straddled the U.S.-Canada border in the St. Lawrence River.

She sank into the soft black leather, watching long stretches of vibrant late spring green grass and leafy trees scroll past her window, a stark and welcome contrast to the brick and concrete vistas that met her daily. Addie breathed it in deeply, relishing the connection to nature, even if it was through a sheet of glass. The little village in Maine where she grew up was near the Acadia

National Forest. Though New York City was where she wanted to be—where she had to be to make her dream of owning a successful Manhattan restaurant come true—she missed the solace of a charming town that shook hands with the natural world around it. It had fed some part of her soul, and that part of her had been starving.

Now she was headed to all the nature she could handle. Soon she would be able to step into the fresh air, surrounded by sun and water. At the thought, eagerness tickled her insides. The reaction surprised her.

Maybe I need a break from the restaurant more than I realized.

'But is this the smart way to do it?' another voice in her head needled.

Addie's pulse quickened. Of course she had misgivings. This whole thing was far out of her comfort zone. She was a planner. A prepper. Anything but spontaneous. Her recipes were researched, tested, revamped, and tested again before incorporating them into the menu. Her shopping was thoroughly investigated live and online before purchasing. She didn't buy a pair of shoes without visiting at least three stores to compare options and prices. Yet, here Addie had taken a total stranger up on a wild offer on the spot. An offer made by a desperate woman, who breezed into the restaurant after midnight, without calling ahead, promising thousands of dollars for a mere four days of work at her home.

In the middle of nowhere.

On a secluded island.

It could have been an ad teaser for a missing-person true-crime podcast.

Gillian had certainly thought so, and told Addie she was crazy for remotely considering it.

But Gillian isn't the one who practically froze to death in the brutal cold snap in March because she had to keep the heat off in her apartment to afford the electric bill.

Yes, the offer was odd and out of the blue, but also an amazing opportunity. Though it undeniably landed in the "too-good-to-be-true" category, Addie couldn't identify anything actually *wrong* with it. Plus, ten thousand dollars went a long way toward offsetting any sketchiness inherent in Monica's proposal.

However, because Addie didn't have a death wish, after getting back from work last night—in truth, early this morning—she checked her gut, prayed about it, and researched Monica online. The woman's social media presence was surprisingly negligible, but the little bit Addie read on her Facebook page and in one or two news articles revealed she was an Upper East Side resident, a philanthropist of the New York art scene, and the wife of Richard Farrow, an executive with a renowned internet security firm.

Monica hadn't been kidding about him being a private person. He had no social media presence and appeared only sparingly in pieces related to Monica's charity work or his firm's achievements. In the end, Addie had drifted to sleep believing the job was too good to pass up and, unless she felt differently when she woke or Monica's references didn't pan out, she was going to do it.

Addie's phone buzzed. Gillian was calling and—not for the first time—Addie wondered if her manager and friend had some kind of sixth sense. She answered, already smiling. "Yes, mother?"

"Very funny," said Gillian, "but if you make decisions like a teenager, I'm going to treat you like one."

"I don't know what you're talking about."

Gillian's exasperated sigh trickled through the phone. "Did you at least check the references?"

"Of course."

"Before you *left*?"

Addie paused a beat. "Couldn't. Too early. But fifteen minutes ago, I got ahold of them and both gave glowing recommendations for the Farrows. Said they couldn't imagine better people to work for."

"And if they had said they were serial killers?"

"Well...suspected or convicted?"

Gillian snorted. "Come on, Addie—"

"Gillian, it's fine. *I'm* fine. Plus, after this weekend I'll have ten thousand more dollars in the bank. I'm having a hard time seeing a downside."

Addie's response was closer to the truth than Gillian probably would have liked. She couldn't imagine learning anything sufficiently troublesome to make it *not* worth ten grand to follow through.

"Call me when you get there. Let me know it's all good."

"I will. I promise," Addie replied.

"I still expect you to live up to your standards. I don't care what they're paying you. Don't be bullied into any ridiculous choices."

"Like what?"

"Like catsup on steak. Ranch dressing on bleu cheese crumbles. Cooking without salt—"

"Okay, okay. I got it."

"You take care of you," Gillian said, a note of seriousness injected into her tone.

"Will do. Talk to you soon."

Addie hung up, stifling a yawn as they continued up I-81 North, out of Binghamton and deeper into Upstate New York. The droning of the car as it rolled along and the sun streaming in, warming the backseat, held her hostage in a lingering state of drowsiness. She craved a vanilla macchiato. She regretted ever trying the things because she was immediately hooked and they were so expensive, something her current budgeting didn't allow for. It was still her first thought when she craved caffeine, but she had switched to

The Offer

regular coffee, cream and sugar, to conserve funds. At the moment, though, she would settle for black and hours-old as long as it was leaded. She presumed the driver would make a detour to find a cup if she asked, but she loathed the idea of delaying their arrival because she had absentmindedly left her travel mug full of a stiff Colombian blend sitting on her kitchen counter.

She leaned forward. "Excuse me, Carl?"

"Ma'am?" His reply was simple and sharp and the first words he had spoken since giving his name when he ushered her into the car back at her apartment. He looked to be in his forties, with a receding hairline and a perpetually grumpy disposition that did not invite conversation. His brusque response only reinforced the perception.

"You don't have any drinks, do you? Caffeinated ones? I left my coffee at home this morning."

He gave the slightest unenthusiastic nod backward. "Cooler on the floor behind me," he said, his tone thick with disdain as if branding her an idiot for not seeing it sooner.

Of course, she *had* noticed it when she got in but assumed it belonged to him because he didn't offer it to her.

So...not aiming for a Mister Congeniality award, hmm, Carl?

Addie opened the sleek black cooler, happy to find it stocked with soda, water, grapes, and assorted cheeses.

"We can make a stop if you want to, but we won't have long," Carl droned, sounding very much like he did not want to stop. "Mrs. Farrow said the ferry would be expecting you."

"No, this is fine." Addie selected a Coca-Cola, cracked it open, and sipped. It wasn't hot, but the icy liquid did the trick, providing a jolt to her system. She could almost feel the rush of sugar and caffeine pouring into her veins. Addie popped a crunchy green grape into her mouth, chased it with another sip, and began to come to life.

They wouldn't reach the town of Clayton, New York, where Addie would catch a boat to Spirits Island, for another three hours. That gave her plenty of time to finish what she had to do. She arranged her iPad, laptop, and Monica's instructions around her in a makeshift workspace and focused on the tasks at hand. For a moment she considered whether she should update anyone else besides Gillian about her trip.

She hadn't told her parents. They would have chided her for taking the job from a stranger and going alone, which was precisely why she didn't tell them. As for friends, well, she didn't see them much these days, so she didn't need to tell them either. They wouldn't even notice she was gone. The realization tweaked her heart. She used to spend at least one weekend day with her buddies, having brunch, exploring Manhattan, or visiting their favorite spots. That had ended in recent months because of the restaurant. Regret stung the way it always did when she dwelled on her self-imposed isolation.

Someday soon it will be better. I'll have more time and it'll go back to the way things were. Dinners out and Sunday afternoons in Central Park.

Yet another reason I can't afford to say no to ten thousand dollars.

Neither was there a boyfriend who would be worried. Her last relationship had been a disaster of monumental proportions, driving her trust in men and interest in dating below a measurable threshold. That truth cut as deep as the truth concerning the state of her friendships.

Enough, Addie. Enough.

Addie jiggled her head as if jostling the cheerless thoughts right out of her skull. Mentally pivoting from the pathetic condition of her social life, she switched on her laptop and got busy.

If she was going to earn her fee, her menus would have to be top-notch. She had brought the ingredients she would need for her signature dishes, the perishables now stored in a cooler in the trunk alongside a few boxes of dry goods. As much as possible, though, she would incorporate whatever had already been bought for her predecessor to limit waste. Monica's packet contained the prior chef's menu and his ingredient list, which Addie had cursorily reviewed after arriving home. Now she studied it in detail. One corner of her mouth rose.

This will work.

Not only was she certain she could use the ingredients and dishes the other chef had planned, she was confident she would be able to put her own spin on them and create something memorable. Something worthy of an unforgettable fiftieth-birthday celebration. One deserving of the ten grand Monica paid.

And one that would give Monica a reason to keep her hinted promise to send business my direction. As compelling as the money was, the future-stream-of-high-dollar-patrons carrot Monica had dangled was every bit as enticing.

Addie sighed contentedly. Four days of cooking culinary delights on the gorgeous waters of the St. Lawrence River, culminating in a much-needed boost to her checking account. A consistently booked dining room and what she expected would be a five-star review from Jonas Cartwright. Bubbly optimism rose in Addie's belly. Things were finally looking up after so many months of struggling.

Her smile stretching into a grin, she dove into her planning.

5

ADDIE

The car came to a stop on Riverside Drive in Clayton, aptly named as the street ran directly alongside the St. Lawrence River bank. From the back seat Addie had a clear view of the greenish-blue water, the wooded islands in the distance, and the homes dotting them.

They parked in front of a boxy two-story structure covered in red clapboard siding and white trim, one of many similar buildings in a variety of colors lining the road. The metal sign above the entrance on the side door read, "Brixton & Sons Waterway Services," in painted letters, and beneath that, "Marina, Taxi, Property Management, and Deliveries."

"Is this it?" Addie asked Carl. Only a couple of cars sat in the parking lot, and there was no one outside. Not to mention there was no ferry in sight. The place felt a little dead for the middle of the day, even though it wasn't the high summer season.

"Yes, ma'am, this is it," Carl answered, the words rolling unenthusiastically off his tongue.

Ahh. The "she's-such-a-dummy" tone reemerges. Love that, Carl.

"I was told to have you go in and ask for Sam," he mumbled. "He knows you're coming. He'll help you with your luggage and the rest."

Addie eyed the back of Carl's head. *Translation, you won't be helping.*

Emitting a resigned sigh, she reached for the door handle, wondering how much Monica was paying Carl and whether she offered bonuses for being rude to riders. If so, Carl was making a killing.

She slipped out of the car and walked to the entrance, which had a plastic "OPEN" sign hanging inside the glass. A tinkling bell announced her arrival as she pushed into a space brimming with boating equipment and supplies of all sorts, including groceries and other sundry items, organized on rows and rows of shelving. It smelled faintly of gasoline or oil or something machinery-oriented. In the background, Jimmy Buffett sang about the beach and flip-flops.

She approached the unmanned counter where a rack displayed flyers describing the multitude of services offered by Brixton & Sons. It seemed this business sold or delivered about anything a person in the islands might need.

"Spreading yourselves a bit thin, aren't you?" Addie mumbled to herself, perusing one of the flyers, then turning it over to read the backside.

"We don't tend to think so," a deep voice answered. Addie's gaze snapped up to a man who had somehow slipped in a door behind the counter without her noticing. He wore a navy T-shirt with the business's logo on it and dark-wash jeans. Stepping closer, he dropped a plastic crate on the countertop where it landed with a tremendous thunk.

"Sorry," Addie said, a shiver of mortification rippling through her. She wiggled the flyer before replacing it in its spot on the rack. "It's just…I thought all of this sounded like a lot for one outfit to take care of."

He tilted his head to the side. "Depends on the outfit, I guess," he said, one corner of his mouth rising into an amused smile, allaying her embarrassment somewhat.

She responded in kind, allowing a smile to peek out. "I guess it does. I'm, um, here to catch a boat to Spirits Island. I'm supposed to ask for Sam?" Her pitch rose, her comment more a question than a statement. "That's what they told me. I'm—"

"Adelaide Nichols. Chef extraordinaire?" He ran a hand through his light-brown wavy hair.

She adopted a grin. "I don't know about extraordinaire, but, yeah, I'm Adelaide—Addie."

"I'm Sam," he said, extending a tanned hand. Addie shook it, noticing his skin was a bit rough, his grip strong. It was the hand of someone who did physical work for a living. She liked that. Her fingers bore their own testament to her career as a chef—scars from the all-too-frequent cuts and burns in the kitchen. Knives and fire were bound to leave their marks. When it occurred to her that they were *still* shaking hands, she retracted hers, heat flushing at the base of her neck.

He checked his watch. "Well, you're right on time. Mrs. Farrow said to expect you around noon." Characterizing her as "on-time" was generous. It was already twelve thirty, making Addie even more grateful they hadn't stopped for coffee on the way.

His eyes slid down to the floor by her feet then back up. "I assume you've got stuff, bags and whatnot?"

"It's out in the car. I can get it. If you'll tell me where to take—"

The Offer

"Nothing doing. I've got it. Part of the service," Sam said, smacking the laminate with an open palm. "I'll be out in a second to load it up." He jerked his head in the direction of the parking lot. "I'll meet you out there," he said, before disappearing through the door behind the counter without waiting for her answer.

Addie headed to the car where Sam appeared a few minutes later with a double-decker cart. Together they transferred the supplies from the trunk. Predictably, Carl didn't offer to help, instead driving away as soon as the last bit was unloaded. Sam took charge of the cart, rolling it to the rear of the building with Addie in tow, pulling her wheeled luggage.

When they rounded the back corner of Brixton & Sons, the view opened up to a marina consisting of three long covered docks jutting out into the river. The majority of the slips were in use, filled with a wide range of styles and sizes of boats. Sam turned down the first dock, the cart rumbling and bumping across the uneven boards. He made an immediate right, heading down the walkway beside the first slip where a good-sized boat was tied up.

"Nice boat," Addie said, admiring the sleek vessel. "What kind is it?"

"She's a thirty-foot walk-around cruiser. Gets the job done." He grabbed a box from the cart and stepped down into the boat to load it. He started to climb out again, but before he could, Addie picked up the next box and gave it to him.

"Thanks," he said, taking it from her and lowering it onto the deck.

"We had one sort of like this when I was growing up in Maine." She presented her cooler of supplies to Sam. "Much smaller, though, and it didn't work most of the time."

"Yeah, that happens a lot with boats." Sam brushed his hands on his jeans. "Of course, that's what keeps us in business." The cart was empty, but he held out his hand again. When she didn't react, he asked, "Your bags?"

"Oh, yeah. Not sure where my head is," Addie said, dragging her suitcase closer. She passed it to him, followed by her duffel. "I didn't get much sleep last night."

Sam stowed each bag, then reached toward her. "Now you," he said, unleashing a smile that crinkled the corners of his eyes.

Something about his smile unsettled her, and Addie sucked in a quiet breath. The best word she could come up with to describe the affecting quality was...dangerous. But not in a "don't-trust-me-I-may-be-a-stalker" way.

Dangerous in the way that, if a girl wasn't careful, she would get roped in by that smile whether she wanted to or not. And Addie didn't want to. She was too busy, too focused, too tired, too jilted... too everything...to even entertain the notion of dating anyone right now. All the same, another millisecond ticked by with Addie staring until her frontal lobe kicked into gear.

What is wrong with you? Step into the stupid boat and stop acting like a thirteen-year-old.

She shoved her hand toward Sam, and he grasped it. Addie stepped down onto the deck, the craft bouncing gently in response to her added weight. His fingers were warm against her skin, the rugged hold they had on hers seemingly advertising that he had everything under control and that as long as she was with him, she didn't have to worry about anything. An annoyed voice in her head rebuked her. *He's not a Marvel character. He's not saving you from a burning house. He's ferrying you to an island. Pull yourself together.*

Obediently, her fingers loosened, but before she managed to let go Sam released his grip, his arms dropping to his sides as he eyed her curiously. "You ready?" he asked, his tone sparkling with amusement.

He can't know what I'm thinking.

Can he?

No. Not possible. But how he was appraising Addie made her wonder if he maybe...*suspected*. Her stomach did a tiny flip at the prospect, as if she had been caught in the act of flirting.

Which she wasn't.

She definitely wasn't.

Addie straightened and brought her chin up, dusting off the proposition and hoping that a little bit of professionalism would put to rest any presumptions of that nature Sam might be harboring.

"Absolutely," she said, lowering herself into the seat opposite the pilot's chair and directing her gaze away from him to the river beyond. "Let's go."

A fine mist sprayed Addie's face as they bounced over the wake, speeding across the waters of the St. Lawrence River. A V-formation of geese flew overhead, black outlines against a brilliant blue sky. As far as she could see in either direction, islands of different sizes spanned the waterway, with houses no less varied—some grand estates, others modest cabins. Some islands had thick woods, boasting dark evergreen pines and firs contrasted with the bright, leafy green of oaks and maples. Others were mere strips of land rising from the water, topped with scrubby grass and a handful of trees. They were tiny kingdoms, cut off from one another and everyone else by the channels of water between them as if isolation had been a crucial ingredient in the recipe for God's creation of this place. She understood the appeal of somewhere to go to be utterly alone. Just you, a house, and an island, the river separating you from whatever parts of the outside world you wanted to escape.

Addie's brief research after getting home from the restaurant that morning—before crashing on her bed, still wearing her work clothes—hadn't yielded any detailed information about Spirits Island. A few of the larger islands had specifics online—like Wellesley Island on the United States side and Wolfe Island in Canada—but most private islands didn't have a profile on the web unless they were available for rent on sites like Vrbo or Airbnb. Addie did manage to pull up a Google Maps photo of the Farrows' island which included a shot of "Number One Spirits Island," their sprawling multi-story Victorian mansion replete with a wraparound porch, turrets and half a dozen chimneys.

Some little vacation home, Addie had thought when the picture popped up on her laptop, concluding Monica's choice of words at the restaurant had fallen far short of doing it justice.

She didn't know a lot about the Thousand Islands region and was surprised to learn Spirits Island was one of the eighteen-hundred-plus islands making up the archipelago in the St. Lawrence River. It straddled the United States-Canadian border along the northwestern edge of New York State. Addie had never visited, though friends had rented a cabin there a couple of years ago. They had raved about it, and now looking at the gorgeous scenery, vast stretches of water, and charming towns on the shore, she understood why.

"It's really beautiful here," Addie yelled over the wind roaring in her ears.

Sam bobbed his head in agreement. "I don't ever get tired of it."

Their course took them zooming past an island with a large, cut-stone house perched on one end. Given the manicured vines growing up all sides, Addie suspected it had been there quite a while and wondered whether it might have been constructed during the Golden Age of the Thousand Islands, back when the high-society elite of the late nineteenth and early twentieth centuries made the region their playground.

The style of the Farrows' house suggested it might have been built in that same period, though Addie would have to ask Monica to be sure. Back then the unfathomably wealthy from New York, Chicago, etcetera, erected mansions—even one castle—establishing the archipelago as a luxury holiday destination. Improvements in the region through the decades by both countries, including an international bridge and a national park, had ensured the area remained a modern-day bustling vacation spot and retreat for people like the Farrows, who owned properties in the islands as second—or third or fourth—homes.

The region had a rich history steeped in the War of 1812, actual piracy, and a fair amount of Prohibition bootlegging, which was responsible for the naming of Whiskey Island. Addie was hoping this was also the story behind Spirits Island, and not a generations-old tale involving a suspected haunting. Not that she believed in ghosts, but she wasn't keen on sleeping overnight in a place with enough bizarre happenings to invoke the supernatural.

The boat bounced on an errant wake from another vessel and Addie gripped the railing, laughing.

"You good?" Sam asked.

Addie nodded. "Fine. Great, actually. I've missed being on the water."

"How long has it been?"

It had been a while. The answer surprised her when she did the math. "Two summers ago. When I went to Maine for my brother Noah's wedding." That weekend the five of them had taken Mom and Dad's boat out—the ancient thing happened to be working—for a quick spin. Speeding over sun-kissed swells while watching the gulls dive for fish with the breeze on her face had been exhilarating. As it was now.

"Is it just you and your brother?"

"No. Noah's the youngest of my four brothers. I was the baby by ten years. Came along late."

"I'll bet no one wanted to date you." When she gave him an odd look, he clarified, "Because of the high risk of ending up with a black eye if things didn't turn out well. You know, brothers and younger sisters."

She did know. All too well. Her older brothers had never stopped treating her like a kid and too often lovingly struggled with taking her seriously. It didn't help that they were all over-achievers who grasped every gold ring they ever reached for. Growing up in their shadows had been daunting, and, if she was honest, fueled her drive to succeed even when that meant operating a restaurant in one of the toughest markets on earth. She wanted to prove she could do what she had set out to do, like they always did. Anything less would feel like failure.

But she didn't want to think about that now. The sun and water and ripple of the air over her skin were too compelling. Addie drank in the sweet sense of liberation, marveling at the realization that she hadn't had a vacation from the restaurant since that time with her siblings two years earlier. Going that long without a real holiday was not healthy. She knew that. Workaholics burned out.

It wasn't as if she didn't want to take a break. Work simply made it too hard to get away. She only had one day off each week—Sunday—because that night tended to be their slowest. One night wasn't enough time to go anywhere.

Maybe her time on Spirits Island would serve as something other than a way to make a fast ten grand. Maybe it would be the mental and physical disconnect she needed more than she cared to admit. Four days of cooking without worrying about filling a dining room with people, the bills stacked on her desk in the back office, or the rent on her apartment due next week.

The rent I'll be able to pay after this.

The thought buoyed her, lifting her spirits like the wind was lifting and tossing the ponytail she had swiftly fashioned when they pulled away from the dock. A smile slipped onto her face and she turned to tell Sam how much she was enjoying the ride.

He sat in the cockpit, his light-brown wavy hair, which fell to right above his shoulders, whipping in the air stream. His eyes were a matching brown, and his skin had a golden cast to it, no doubt due to the hours he likely spent in the sunshine ferrying people like he was ferrying her now. How old was he? Close to her age? Maybe a few years older at most. It wasn't lost on her that it had been ages since she bothered to take stock of someone in this way.

Before she managed to say anything about the ride, Sam's gaze flitted to her, and he caught Addie staring at him. Her cheeks flashed hot, her stomach dropping at the thought of how pink her face must be. Attempting to redirect him to something less mortifying, she gestured at the boat. "So, um...how long have you been doing this?"

"My whole life. I'm the 'sons' in Brixton & Sons. Or—" He gave a slight tilt of his head. "—one of them, anyway. My brother, Jep, is back at the marina. He mainly handles the in-shop repairs."

"How much do you deal with the Farrows?"

"On and off as needed."

"What do you know about them? I mean, I'm not prying for the sake of prying," she qualified, justifying herself. "They're strangers and this was a last-minute job offer. It's a little unsettling going in blind."

He shrugged. "They're nice enough. Mr. Farrow's owned Spirits Island for ten years or so, I guess. Mrs. Farrow's been around for seven or eight."

"Second wife?"

"Third, I think. But I try not to ask too many questions. Not good for business." He winked at her.

"Oh. Right. Hint taken."

"No, that's...that's not what I meant. I might not ask *them* questions, but I don't mind you asking me. Fire away."

"Well...I'd appreciate anything that gives me a better idea of what they're like. So I know what to expect."

He looked thoughtful as if trying to formulate an appropriate answer. "I've only dealt with them in a professional context. I wouldn't call them friendly, but I wouldn't say rude either."

Not a very detailed description, but I can cope with "not rude."

She had coped with worse.

He cut a fleeting glance at her before directing his attention ahead again. "Will you have any extra time on your hands while you're here?"

Addie's brow scrunched. Surely he wasn't considering asking her out during her stay.

He must have picked up on her confusion because he immediately followed up with, "I only ask because, if you will, you should check into the local tours. Some are very good. They go into the history of the area and specific islands, and sometimes the houses if they have good stories tied to them." He reached into his pocket, extracted a business card, and extended it to her. "If you decide to squeeze one in, let me know and I can set something up for you, or make a delivery if you need something. Text or call and I'll come as soon as I can. Or Jep will. It's usually not long if we're close by."

"Travel agent, delivery service, and taxi," she said, tucking the card away to keep the wind from stealing it. A grin tugged at the edges of her mouth. "Your brochure didn't lie."

"Nope."

"Well, thank you, but I won't have time for anything but work. And I wouldn't feel right about taking time for myself, anyway."

"Hold on to it just in case. Normally the Farrows would be able to give you a ride in a pinch, but I happen to know their boat is down at the moment. We're supposed to take a look at it when we can fit it in. Though, even if it was working," he said, his eyebrows rising, "you'd still want that card. You'd be surprised how often guests end up stranded on these islands when they have a falling out with their host or the host has too much to drink and can't drive when somebody needs to leave."

"Really?"

"Crazy situations. Some you wouldn't believe."

Addie didn't like the sound of that. "You're not suggesting that might happen with the Farrows?"

His eyes cut to hers. "No. Not at all." He tossed his head, shaking the hair out of his eyes. "I'm just aware it happens. Better to be safe than stuck."

"Okay. Good to know." She leaned back in the seat. "So how far is it to the island?"

Sam pursed his lips, his chin jutting forward. "We've been gone, what, five minutes?" He glanced down at his watch, then locked eyes with her. "I'd say thirty more seconds," he said, grinning and pointing starboard.

Addie followed his finger to a heavily-wooded island about fifty yards to their right where, up the sloped grass from its shore, a plum-colored Victorian mansion rose majestically, its chimneys and turrets reaching toward the azure sky.

6

ADDIE

The dock at Spirits Island consisted of a large boathouse and two covered slips. One held a boat—the term "yacht" seemed more appropriate—the size of Sam's plus half. Addie presumed this was the non-working vessel belonging to the Farrows. Sam pulled into the empty slip and tied off. Addie hopped out and helped him unload, accepting items as he passed them over. He insisted on handling the last few heavy bits, so Addie grabbed her bags and walked to the end of the dock beside the boathouse and took it all in.

The island was a striking mass of emerald against the dazzling sapphire of the day's cloudless sky. The woods stretched so far on either side of the house that she couldn't see where they ended. They were so dense it was also impossible to discern how deep the island was from this perspective. A meticulously landscaped path led from the boathouse up to a large clearing extending from the shore to the house and the manicured grounds immediately surrounding it. The plum-painted, white-trimmed, five-story beauty Addie had seen online towered above it all.

Five stories. Wow. Or, at least five. Maybe more if there's a cellar.

Stone masonry sheathed the foundation. Lavender wood-plank siding, snowy trim, and charcoal gray shingles covered the rest of the house. Intricate scrollwork and fashioned railing spindles added special touches. Massive porches wrapped around both the first and second stories. She expected that the dormers and ornate turrets scattered along the structure provided stunning vistas, particularly on the highest floors and especially at sunrise and sunset. The house was situated such that the front and both sides had panoramic views of the water. The rear grounds were hidden by a compact row of tall evergreens serving as a privacy hedge.

There was something dark-fairy-tale-esque about the house. For all its beauty and delicate touches, its countless steps and porches inviting you in, something about the house seemed...untrustworthy. Not unlike the Grimm Brothers' story of Hansel and Gretel and the appealing house of bread, cake, and sugar intended to lure them to their doom. The odd sensation pricked her like a warning. Like her gut was trying to tell her something.

Sam appeared at her elbow, rolling up with the cart laden with her supplies. "The island's a decent size as the private ones go," he said, looking up at the house. "One of the more literally 'private' ones, thanks to thick woods covering pretty much all of it except the house and surrounding grounds." He spiraled a hand in the air, gesturing at the trees. "Some of the houses are exposed in every direction, but not this one. It has a guest cottage too, over there somewhere, hidden back inside that tree line." Sam pointed to the wooded area to the left of the house. "Old caretaker's house or something."

He started pulling the cart toward the house, turning to walk backward so he faced her as he went. It was a bumpy trek, given the natural growth of grass between the large flagstones making up the path. "I'm going to the kitchen entrance at the back," he said, jerking his head at the right side of the house. "They'll want me to unload this stuff there. You can meet me when you're done."

"Done with what?" she asked, following him and dragging her luggage behind her, having to give it a good pull every several feet when the wheels hit the gaps between the stones. "Shouldn't I come with you?"

"Can't imagine they would want you coming in around the back. You should head on up to the front door. First impressions and all that."

He was right. Of the two Farrows, she had only met Monica and she'd never been to the house. Was it more professional to introduce herself by way of the front door? Then again…why did she care? This was silly. She wasn't about all this proper…whatever. Front, back…it didn't matter. But since Monica hadn't said, she would take Sam's advice. He might not know them well, but he knew them better than she did. "I'll have to take your word for it," Addie said, diverting her steps to follow the path that led to the porch.

"I'll see you in the kitchen in a minute," he called out, "unless they hold you up, because I've got to get back. If I have to go, I'll leave everything inside where you can find it."

Before Addie could decide whether she ought to say goodbye in case she didn't get the chance in the house, Sam was already well down the other path. Sighing, she tightened her grip on her suitcase and continued in the other direction, following the flagstones that ended at a full flight of steps which bypassed the first floor, ascending all the way to the second-story porch. As she mounted the white stairs, nervous butterflies zoomed around her stomach. Annoyed, she pressed a hand against her midsection.

The Offer

Stop it!

She shouldn't be the least bit nervous about a gig like this. Private catering for two was nothing compared to what she did at the restaurant six nights a week. What was her problem?

It's the unfamiliarity of it all. The last-minute nature of it.

Though her thoughts drifted to the gingerbread house tale again, she pushed down her misgivings and summoned her resolve.

"You'll be fine," she whispered to herself. "For ten thousand dollars and a paid four-day vacation from East to West, you'll be *fine*. So, go ahead nerves, give it your best shot. We aren't leaving without that payday."

She took a deep breath, ran a hand over her windswept hair, and rang the doorbell. Mellow gong tones echoed over the porch as she straightened and pasted on a pleasant smile. Heavy steps sounded from within. A shadow appeared through the warbled glass panes set in the white door. The lock clicked and the door swung open.

Addie's heart went cold. One hand moved to the door frame, pushing against it for stability as her shell-shocked brain worked to process what she was seeing.

Forget ten thousand dollars.

Ten million wouldn't be enough to make her stay on that island one single second longer.

7

ADDIE

Her throat was a scorched desert. Her mind a fog at sea, enveloping everything, affording no bearing. Her body a matchstick statue, threatening collapse.

"Rob?" The word escaped her lips, a rough whisper that exhausted the last bit of air in her seized lungs.

In the doorway stood a man dressed in a Ralph Lauren pullover and khakis. His hair lay in medium-length waves, salt and pepper in color, the ends turning up at the base of his neck. His piercing eyes, more gray-blue than she remembered, narrowed sharply at the sight of her, fear igniting behind them.

With two fluid steps, he moved onto the porch and delicately pulled the door shut. "What are you doing here?" he asked, his tone brittle and hushed.

The question, directed like an accusation, like a parent scolding a child, sparked fiery indignation within her. Addie found her voice.

The Offer

"What am *I* doing here? I was invited. Hired to cater for this house this weekend. What are *you* doing here?"

He shot a look back at the door as if checking to see if anyone was there. All Addie saw through the marbled glass were still shadows and amorphous shapes of color. He swiveled back to her.

"We don't have much time," he started, urgency thrusting his words at her. He pressed a hand against her forearm, pushing her backward, closer to the edge of the porch. "She'll be here any minute. I—"

"Rob—"

"It's Richard."

Richard.

As in Richard Farrow.

Addie's mouth dropped, despite that the last thing she would consciously want was to let him see emotion of any kind from her—at least any emotion other than righteous anger. But this...revelation...was too much, and the foggy sensation of earlier returned as the truth sank in. A faint ringing in her ears joined the lightheadedness sweeping over her.

This was wrong. He was wrong. She found her voice again, though what came out didn't sound like hers at all. "What?" she managed, the word guttural, almost a growl, bitterness biting off the end.

"My name. It's Richard, not Rob. Whatever you do, don't call me Rob."

No, no, no. It can't be.

As if someone pressed play on a black-and-white reel of her memories from her last relationship, scenes began flashing in Addie's mind and everything started to make horrible sense.

All his excuses. His bizarre behavior. The inconsistent calls and the eleventh-hour cancelations. Gillian had tried to tell her. Even though her friend had suspected from the beginning that something was off, Addie, charmed by his ways and relishing having someone in her life after being alone for so long, ignored Gillian. Addie ignored the red flags too. She disregarded the signs and symptoms until it was so bad, she wasn't able to pretend it was a normal, much less healthy, relationship, and ended it. She hadn't seen or heard from him again. Until now.

The ringing in her head grew louder.

What a fool she had been. She had chosen to believe he was merely selfish. A distracted boyfriend consumed by work. Gillian had always insisted there was more to the story. Her smart, perceptive friend had been right. Right about the reasons Rob was...the way he was. Waves of embarrassment over being so gullible and anger over his betrayal surged alongside one another in her chest, the volume of her voice cresting with them.

"You're *married*?" she finally got out. "I mean, Gillian thought, maybe...but, I said, no! I *defended* you! But...you're married? That's the reason for all of it?"

He splayed his hands and jabbed them at her, motioning for her to hush. She took another step back, pressed her lips together, as if sealed by glue, and waited for whatever answer he thought would redeem him.

Instead, he shrugged as if what she had said was the least consequential truth ever unearthed, eyeing her like she was an idiot for not figuring it out sooner. "Uh...yeah."

She had to resist the urge to slap him.

For a moment she stared at him, biting the inside of her cheek. He was not having a normal response to the situation. He should be more upset. Embarrassed. Appalled at being found out.

He wasn't. Because it wasn't a big deal for him. *She* hadn't been a big deal to him.

"So who is Rob Franklin?"

He shook his head, looked back toward the door again, and

leaned in conspiratorially. "Doesn't exist. It's a name I use sometimes when...well, when I need one that isn't mine." His lips formed a hard line.

I'm not even the first one.

Addie swallowed the lump in her throat. "Does she know?"

Richard shook his head again, then silently watched her, seemingly gauging her reaction. What was he waiting for? For her to scream? Cry? Yell out for Monica and spill the whole sordid story? She didn't blame him for wondering what she was going to do next. She didn't know either. "This is insane. Monica...*your wife*...hired me for this weekend. To cater. *For you.* As a surprise for your birthday."

"Well," he started, one corner of his lips rising wryly, "mission accomplished."

Addie's jaw dropped, her mouth forming an "O." "Wha—You're not—How can you joke about—"

"Look," he said, clasping her arm, "we don't have time for this now." As if underlining his point, the sound of light, clicking steps came from somewhere beyond the front door.

She made her decision. Not that she had any other choice. "I'm not staying," Addie said. "Sam's in the kitchen, dropping off my supplies. I'll go wait in the boat and catch a ride back with him. Tell Monica I got sick or something. I don't care. I'll return the money to her—"

"You can't leave," he said, his grip intensifying. "You can't. She'll be suspicious. She'll have been in the kitchen by now and Sam will have told her you're here. If you go now, it'll create a world of hurt for me."

"Good," Addie retorted bitterly, shaking off his hand and stepping back from him. Why he would think she would save him was beyond her. A man who had lied to her about everything. He had made her a party to something sordid. She was never more grateful that they had only dated for a matter of weeks, but still, her stomach soured at the thought.

I should march inside and lay it all out for Monica right now.

"No, not good," Richard answered. "It'll kill Monica. Regardless of what you think of me, don't do that to her. Just don't."

The clicking steps sounded closer and were now paired with a red, lanky shape visible through the glass and looming larger by the second.

He looked over his shoulder at the approaching figure, then turned back to Addie. His gaze was fierce, but also now—to her astonishment—pleading, all former overtones of nonchalance gone. "*Please.* Go with it for now. I'll explain everything when we have a minute. You don't understand. More is at stake than you realize."

The figure reached the door. An arm stretched toward the handle.

"I'm begging you, Addie. Give me the chance to explain or you'll ruin—"

The door swung open before he managed to finish his sentence.

8

ADDIE

"Chef Nichols!" Monica squealed, sashaying forward to hug Addie like an old friend. Addie tensed, stiff as a scarecrow. Monica wasn't fazed and squeezed before releasing her. She stepped back and playfully swiped at Richard's forearm. "You're terrible. She was supposed to be a surprise."

Richard shuffled in place and chuckled as if the last three minutes on the porch hadn't happened. "She is. You told me we weren't expecting anyone this weekend."

"No, I mean, a surprise I presented at dinner tonight. I was going to have her come *through the back*," Monica said, directing her words to Addie, along with a chastising gaze. Her unnaturally long, fake eyelashes fluttered, her smile a bit too taut to be believable.

That's what she's annoyed about? "Sorry," Addie started, "I...Sam said...I didn't see in your instructions—"

Monica waved her off, her red nails rippling. "Doesn't matter. It's probably my fault." Her tone made it clear she didn't truly think that at all. "I thought I put it in the instructions, but...well, you're here now."

"Okay," Addie said, her mind attempting to stay present in the conversation, process everything that had happened before Monica opened the door, *and* find an excuse to justify going back home. As her thoughts whirred, she registered Sam in her peripheral vision, heading back down the path to the dock.

Addie wanted to run after him. She wanted to leave the Farrows standing at their door and take off without a word, pulling her bags behind her. She wanted to jump in Sam's boat and speed away like an escape scene out of a movie, leaving the Farrows on the porch, helpless to follow.

Instead, she stood there, turning to watch Sam, who gave a quick wave before boarding his boat.

Richard's voice pulled her back to them. "It *is* a real surprise," he said in that rich voice of his. The one he used when he was being charming. Plying you. The voice she had known for weeks as Rob Franklin's voice. Someone who didn't exist. "She won't tell me who she is. Said to wait for you."

Monica's eyes cut to Addie's, and she thought she saw a flash of approval at this reaction. She held out a hand toward Addie, like Vanna White revealing a letter. "I thought you'd recognize her, as you said it was one of your new favorite restaurants."

Richard's eyebrows rose, calling for more information.

"This is Adelaide Nichols, the chef at East to West. I've hired her for the weekend. Happy birthday!" She threw her hands out like a cheerleader after a stunt, then snatched them in again, clasping them against her chest. "Do you like it?"

Addie's stomach twisted into an even tighter knot at being referred to as an "it." A thing. A thing specially served up for Richard.

The Offer

I can't do this.

The words echoed through her like a scream let loose on a mountain, though on the outside she remained silent. Staring. What could she say to get out of this? What excuse wouldn't bring Monica's world crashing down and not make her look unprofessional? She was here already and she didn't look or sound sick. Although on second thought, if she stopped trying to hide how she actually felt at the moment she *would* look sick—

Sam's boat engine roared to life. Addie rotated to look fleetingly at him again. He was driving away. Along with her chance to leave.

"Chef Nichols has an *amazing* menu planned for the weekend, and you and I are going to be completely spoiled," Monica said. Addie turned back around to see Monica rise up on the toes of the four-inch heels and peck Richard on the cheek. "But mostly you. You deserve it."

"It's a wonderful present," Richard said, putting his arm around his wife. "Thank you."

How was he doing this? How was he acting like nothing was wrong? That the woman he had dated for weeks wasn't standing on his porch?

In front of his wife.

Sam's boat was a speck on the river now, but she still had his business card in her pocket. If she decided to leave, Addie could reach out and have him come get her. Once she figured out how to handle this. Because right now her addled brain couldn't see a way out.

Monica looked so happy. So content as Richard smiled at her. Sympathy for the duped woman overcame Addie. She might not particularly like Monica—her high and mighty manner wouldn't win her any congeniality awards, and Monica referring to her as an "it" only amplified Addie's distaste. Still, Addie didn't want to be the one to ruin everything. Not that level of ruin, anyway. Ruining a birthday weekend by leaving, she could do. Ruining a marriage, not so much.

Addie had to do this the right way. She needed to think. She needed to know what Richard was alluding to when he said she didn't understand because Addie thought it was pretty obvious what was going on. And she needed to know what he meant when he said something more—something besides this sham of a marriage—was at stake.

Whatever his answers, she was certain she wasn't going to like them.

Entering the house was like walking into a waking nightmare.

Addie followed Monica and Richard into the foyer, then into a living room bigger than her entire apartment, as two conversations took place at once. One conversation outside her head was a continuation of pleasantries, ending with Richard saying he would leave them to it. After eyeing Addie meaningfully, he disappeared down one of several hallways leading further into the house.

The second conversation, one happening totally inside her head, was with herself. Her instincts demanded that she do whatever it took to get out of there. Immediately. Post-haste. Lamentably, her instincts offered no suggestion about how to make that happen without causing all kinds of collateral damage.

Monica instructed Addie to drop her luggage by the stairs, noting they would be back for it in a minute. She gestured for Addie to follow her and embarked on a tour of the main floor, pointing out the various rooms and describing where Addie would find things she might need. Monica's voice filtered into Addie's brain as if by way of a stringed soup can held to Addie's ear. The slight ringing persisted too, which was fitting, given how shell-shocked she was.

The Offer

Despite the emotional blitzkrieg she had just suffered, Addie couldn't help but be impressed by the sheer size of the house. The living spaces were open and airy. Windows were everywhere, offering views of the water on one side and the woods beyond in the back. As for the kitchen...well, it would rival the best she had seen in Manhattan.

"Ten thousand square feet-plus," Monica commented at one point, brushing off the massive measurement with another swirl of her wrist as if that kind of footage was commonplace. "The house was built by the owner of a slew of coal mines back in the day. Or so I'm told," she explained. "Though I suspect he had more going on than legitimate coal operations."

"The bootlegging stories?" Addie prompted.

Monica nodded. "History's not my thing, but, yes. All I know is I had to move heaven and earth to obtain permission to take out interior walls to open up the spaces. You should have seen the size of the kitchen before." Monica shook her head. "Protected historical building, you know. Huge nuisance," she said, her mouth turning down.

While the bones of the house were delightful, the decor was, well...awful. The first floor was decorated in urban, contemporary furnishings, with heavy doses of black-and-white splashed with red accents. The modern art and bold sculpted pieces fashioned from metal, plastic and other cold mediums were glaringly incongruous with the style of the house. The whole thing felt like a crime scene, where tastefulness itself had been murdered. That was before one considered how badly the interior color choices clashed with the lavender paint on the exterior. Addie assumed some kind of historical protection must have prevented Monica from repainting the outside. Or renovating the house altogether.

Their decorator should be shot.

"The art is Richard's passion," Monica noted. "I know it doesn't fit with the house per se, but he insisted on it. At least he let me make the rest of the decorating decisions."

Addie choked back a snort, managing to turn it into an exaggerated cough that she hoped she pulled off. Monica didn't seem to notice.

Their path back through the living room took them past a glossy ebony sofa table adorned by frames holding photographs of two young adults and one boy. Other than the many framed ones of Monica displayed all over the place, and the handful of Richard, they were the first photographs of other people Addie had seen. She paused beside them, leaning in for a better look.

"Are these..." Addie started, then stopped herself. Monica hadn't mentioned having her own children. It might be dangerous to guess who these people were. It was a minefield she didn't want to pick her way over. The boy could conceivably be Monica's. His age made sense, but, the adults? She was still trying to decide how to ask without risking offense when Monica piped in.

"Yes. The children," Monica said, walking back to Addie. She pointed to the photo of a young woman with thin gray-blue eyes and stringy, strawberry-blond-streaked hair. "That's Keeley," she said, her fingertip next aiming at a photo of a young man with the same coloring, "and her brother, Justin. Richard's kids." She sighed disapprovingly. "From his first wife, an absolutely horrible person, by the way. They're both grown and gone. But this"—her lips pulled a smile as she ran a finger over the largest of the three frames—"is Baker. Our angel. He was only six when this was taken, but he's turning eight soon." The platinum-haired boy was grinning, one tooth missing in the front and a smattering of freckles across his cheekbones. Monica inhaled through her nose and straightened. "Such a good boy. Off at Keller taking on the world."

"Keller?" Addie asked.

Monica's brow furrowed and she clicked her tongue derisively.

The Offer

"Keller Institute for Boys? It's a premier boarding school in Upstate New York."

"Oh. Right." Addie had never heard of it. There was no reason for her to keep up with fancy boarding schools in the Northeast. Her gaze went to the photo again, and the boy's impish smile tweaked a nerve in Addie's heart. It seemed a tough way to grow up, being sent off at such a young age. Coming home only for vacations. Essentially being raised by school personnel. Had that been the story for Richard's older children as well?

A question surfaced as Addie looked at the photographs. She thought Monica had indicated that she and her…husband—Addie's stomach tanked at the word—would be the only diners over the weekend. Now, looking at the photographs, she was second-guessing her memory. Had she missed something?

"It's only the two of you I'm cooking for, correct? I mean, it's not a problem if there are others. I've brought more than enough—"

"No, no one else is coming. It's just us." She tapped the boy's photo. "We would have loved to have had Baker here, but with school still in session, it wasn't possible. Of course, Keeley and Justin won't be here. Keeley's off doing her social media influencing thing, or personal-assisting some Hollywood B-lister, or scriptwriting, or whatever her career of the month is," Monica said, rolling her eyes. "I mean, those aren't even really jobs, you know? And Justin…"

She paused, cleared her throat, and shook her head dismissively. "Well, truthfully, I have no idea what Justin's up to. He's a bit of an oddball. Geek Squad candidate if you know what I'm saying. Last year he took a job in Alabama of all places, doing something for some tech company. But, honestly, *Alabama*."

Every time this woman opened her mouth, Addie liked her less. She wondered what Monica's reaction would be if she shared that her mother was originally from Alabama. Maybe she should tell her and Monica would be so annoyed she would ask Addie to leave. That would solve everything.

Unfortunately, nothing was ever that easy.

"Justin said it was too far to come for just a few days, and that he's too busy anyway." She appeared to dwell on that thought for a couple of seconds, then made an abrupt about-face from the sofa table. "Come on. Let's finish the tour and then I'll take you to your room. Usually, I'd have Tanya—our housekeeper—do it, but I wanted to keep things simple this weekend. Give Richard his privacy. So I didn't ask her to be here."

Yeah. Richard's big on privacy, all right.

The floor they were on now, the level accessed from the front door, was the second story. Monica took her down to the first floor, which consisted of a spa replete with a steam room, sauna and hot tub, game room, movie room, and access to the covered porch leading to the pool in the back. Addie was pretty sure Monica had a hand in decorating that floor too. It was as awful as the living room.

They went back to the stairs on the main level, collected Addie's luggage—or rather, Addie collected it—and started up, Monica still chattering away. "With the help out this weekend, we're on our own in the service department. But, we'll manage. That'll fall a bit on you, I'm afraid. You'll need to serve meals as well as prepare them." Monica paused on a step and turned back to face Addie, her features scrunched in mock penitence, her bottom lip poking out like a teenager asking Daddy for more allowance. "I know I didn't mention it when we spoke, but you won't mind, will you? I know it's not something chefs do, buuuut..." Monica strung the word out, letting the unfinished sentence linger in the air, the ten thousand dollars Addie had been paid left unspoken, but distinctly implied.

"No," Addie said. "I won't mind."

That's the last thing about this arrangement that bothers me.

A brilliant smile composed of two rows of expertly-whitened

teeth replaced the pout in what was manifestly a practiced effort. "Excellent," she said, patting Addie's arm condescendingly before tromping upward again, her heels stabbing each step as she went. "Let's get you to your room and then to the kitchen where you can start working your magic."

9

ADDIE

In the third-floor bedroom that was hers for the weekend, Addie flopped back on the wrought iron four-poster bed, with its white linen duvet and fluffy pillows. Unlike most of the rooms, the decor upstairs was in keeping with the period style of the house. For whatever reason, Monica hadn't gotten her hands on it yet. Or perhaps, Richard hadn't let her. Either way, the furnishings were much better suited to the Victorian beauty.

"Part of the guest wing," Monica had explained before leaving Addie to settle in, telling her she would be down in the kitchen and to come find her when she was done. Addie imagined Monica's nails drumming on the granite countertops as she waited impatiently for her to join her, but Addie needed a minute.

She stared at the ceiling fan above her, the blades going round and round like her mind. "What have I gotten myself into?" she asked herself for the umpteenth time since Richard had opened the front door. Thirty minutes after the shock of seeing him in the doorway, she still didn't have an answer.

She had not laid eyes on Richard for two months and, after that night, she had never expected to see him again. New York City was a big place and, although he had frequented her restaurant during their short relationship, as far as she knew, he hadn't set foot inside it after she broke things off.

They had gone to dinner at Le Triomphe on the Upper West Side. She hadn't wanted to go. She had already made up her mind to end it and didn't want to drag it out or be unfair to him. Before she could say anything, he had called up, insisting they meet, pleading that he wanted to make it all up to her—convince her he wasn't the worst boyfriend ever. She decided it would be better to tell him face to face. He was aware she was not happy with the way things had been going between them, but apparently, he hadn't sensed what she was planning. Either that, or he had hoped the charm of the candlelight and crystal would change her mind.

It didn't.

They hadn't been there long before he confronted her about how quiet she was. "Come on, Addie," he had whined dramatically, reaching out to lay a hand on her forearm. "It's not *that* bad. I told you, I've been busy."

She had pulled her arm back, resting it in the lap of her black dress. "And I told you, 'busy' isn't a good enough excuse. Not when you use it every other day."

"Excuse? Excuse for what? We've only been dating six weeks. I'm not sure I need an *excuse*—"

She remembered the indignation that sparked in her belly at his words. "That's what I'm talking about. We've only been dating six weeks. If you're already too busy for me, then, frankly, you're too busy." She had sighed, tired of arguing. She wasn't interested in trying to win him over. Her goal was to end their relationship amicably. "It's fine, Rob. This simply isn't what I'm looking for."

Initially, she thought he might be *exactly* what she was looking for. Older men weren't her go-to when it came to dating, but, for some time now, the men her age she had gone out with had been flaky, aimless, or self-consumed. Rob was forty-two. She hoped at that stage he would be more down-to-earth. Reliable. Settled and more focused. More about things that were real.

"Forty-two," Addie grumbled derisively, grabbing a pillow and clutching it to her chest. The man was turning fifty. He had even lied about his age. That wasn't even the worst thing he had lied about. She was right about him being settled. He was settled, all right. As in *settled down*. She had also been dead wrong about the reliability factor.

His unreliability had been the main red flag. Despite his insistence that he wanted nothing more than to spend time with her, he somehow seldom managed to do it. They had only a dozen dates during their weeks together and she had moved heaven and earth to make those happen, given her crazy schedule at the restaurant. At first she had been swept off her feet with the flowers he sent, the fancy meals, and the limos—all on top of a gold pendant one month in—but she had quickly grown tired of his cancelations. She saved her nights off for him and made plans with him during her daytime off-hours, only to have him abort with little or no notice. He blamed it on traveling for his job as a high-end IT consultant and last-minute rush jobs. She didn't care what the reasons were. It had become obvious they weren't a good fit.

She wasn't bitter about it at all. These things happened. But instead of taking it well, he became argumentative. He went all frosty, his features hardening as he switched gears and began claiming she was the one to blame for their relationship souring,

The Offer

that she had taken advantage of him. He accused her of milking him all those weeks with no intention of sticking around.

Addie remembered being unable to speak, shocked into silence at his nerve. She had brought the pendant with her to return it to him, feeling it wasn't right to keep it. In that heated moment, she had flung it at him. It landed in his soup, splashing red bisque down the front of his starched white shirt, drawing the attention of the other diners.

She had stormed out, leaving him sitting at the table, cursing and ineffectually swiping at the stains with a napkin. That was the last image she had of him. Until tonight when he opened that door.

Now, that same man—Rob or Richard or whatever his name was—was somewhere in this house. The man who had lied to her over and over. Addie squeezed her eyes shut at the thought. More than ever she was grateful they hadn't dated very long or seriously.

"God, tell me what to do," she uttered at the ceiling. "I'm lost here."

Addie closed her eyes and listened to her gut, hoping some brilliant excuse for leaving would miraculously come to her. Something that wouldn't raise questions or frustrate Monica. Monica could make a lot of problems for the restaurant if she wanted to, and something about the woman told Addie she would take to that challenge like a sport.

But the only thing she heard was the whirring of the fan. Addie pulled Sam's card from her pocket and ran her finger around its edge. She would stay on the island long enough to hear Richard's explanation of what else was "at stake" besides his marriage. Afterward, she would insist he help her come up with a reason for leaving that Monica would accept—if not happily, then at least not angrily. She would text Sam to come pick her up and she would leave.

Nothing Richard had to say would change that.

10

NOT ADDIE

And now, ladies and gentlemen, we have live streaming.
The video feed was crystal clear. Adelaide Nichols was lying on her bed, staring at the ceiling. Her face was twisted in concern, her distress evident.

The greeting at the door had to have unnerved her.

So much the better.

After all the brainstorming, the scheming, the endless nights of thinking it through—the plan was working.

Everything was falling into place. No one suspected a thing. Not yet.

Of course, eventually, they would realize what was happening. But by then it would be too late.

Much, much too late.

11

ADDIE

It had been hours. Hours in the kitchen, organizing and prepping for the weekend, and preparing the evening's courses. And still no sign of Richard Farrow. Not one glance inside the room to let Addie know he hadn't forgotten about her. No text. Not even an emoji.

He was avoiding her. Just like when they had dated.

He's got until after dinner, Addie thought, her insides steaming like the pots on the stove. *Then I'm out of here, good excuse or not.* She knew her frustration was getting the best of her. That leaving might be akin to professional suicide, but with every passing second, she cared less and less.

The one saving grace of the last few hours had been the kitchen itself. It was a chef's dream, gleaming with stainless steel and a glossy tile backsplash. An oversized white-and-black marble island held an enormous farmhouse sink. The inset refrigerator was fronted with panels resembling the cabinetry. There was a separate Sub-Zero freezer. From the looks of it, no expense had been spared, including the thousands that would have been spent on the gorgeous, royal-blue La Cornue gas range with gold accents. The made-by-hand French beauty was the most stunning of its kind Addie had ever seen. At six feet, the stove was wider than she was tall. A stab of envy pierced her chest. She would likely never be able to personally afford this degree of culinary luxury.

At least one upside of this tragic weekend is that I get to cook on one of these.

She consoled herself with the thought before taking a sip from the gilt-edged teacup that had belonged to her grandmother. The two of them used to sip tea while she watched her Nana cook. It was a treasured memory of the person who first taught her to love food and the act of preparing it for others. When her Nana passed, Addie inherited the cups and the matching miniature teapot. Now her ritual was to use them while cooking if at all possible. She found it kept her calm when things became chaotic in the kitchen. Like the few other off-site gigs she had catered in the past, she had carefully packed and brought them with her to the island.

Good thing, too. I can't imagine needing calming more than I will this weekend.

The subject of keeping things calm turned Addie's thoughts to Gillian, who had sent multiple texts after she arrived, asking for details. Once Monica finally left Addie alone in the kitchen, she replied to Gillian, but only told her she was safe and all was good. She didn't want to go into the ugly details. It would only spark more questions than she wanted to answer at the moment. Addie would explain it all to Gillian once she got home. For now, it would have to keep.

The Offer

Addie checked her phone again, just to be sure Gillian hadn't texted back. There was nothing new, so she must have been satisfied with the previous response.

It was almost six.

It'll be time to serve the appetizer course soon.

Addie drained her cup and set it aside. Monica had made doubly sure Addie knew they preferred dinner at seven thirty. She had flounced in about an hour ago to remind her of that and to sample the prosciutto Addie was using for the prosciutto-wrapped asparagus hors d'oeuvres. Monica had also stuck her finger into the still-simmering roasted pumpkin and kale soup, then stole a chanterelle mushroom intended for the sauce accompanying the seared Wagyu beef.

After pronouncing it all "divine," Monica made the first of what ended up being two pre-dinner gimlets. That was something else Monica had sprung on Addie when she first came down to meet Monica in the kitchen. She had asked Addie if, since the maid wasn't working that weekend, she would also serve as bartender. Addie's knowledge of cocktail mixing was rather limited, so with an exaggerated sigh, Monica had shown her how to make the few drinks they would be asking for, jotting down the instructions on Addie's iPad. It seemed Monica would go to any lengths to avoid lifting a finger to serve herself over the next few days. After insisting mixing drinks wasn't any different than mixing a cake—which was *so* not true—and that a chef would be able to handle it without any problem, she watched Addie make her gimlet and pronounced it passable before disappearing with it into the belly of the house.

Addie checked the progress of the mushroom sauce and, deciding she had a few moments to spare before the next steps were called for, walked across the kitchen to a seating area with windows facing the rear of the property. A pool backed up to the house, and beyond that, a semi-circle of thick evergreen and deciduous trees blocked it all from the view of anyone outside the area. The result was a luxurious glen, an oasis of sparkling blue water, and all manner of greens from tree-top to the grass carpet. How far the woods extended, and how far away the shore was on that side, she couldn't tell. Whatever lay beyond wasn't visible from this vantage point.

Maybe I can see the water on that side from the tower room.

Addie hadn't been up there yet, but when giving her the tour, Monica had pointed out the stairs leading to it. She would have to investigate later. The ding of her timer broke through her musings, and she walked back to the stove to check the asparagus. They were perfect. She sighed.

I guess it's time to put on a show.

Addie wasn't sure how she was going to survive being in and out of the same room with Richard and Monica for the entire length of dinner. All the more, since Richard hadn't given the slightest indication he was going to follow through with explaining the situation as promised. She was beginning to suspect no explanation was forthcoming, and Richard was simply stringing her along until it was too late to leave.

One by one, Addie arranged the asparagus on a tray, kicking herself for taking Monica Farrow up on an offer that seemed too good to be true at the time, and now had proven it was.

Two and a half hours later, Addie tromped up the stairs, wanting to scream. Dinner had gone off without a hitch. It had also gone off without any acknowledgment by Richard that he had some explaining to do.

Instead, he had been exceedingly pleasant, raving about the

appetizers, the main course, and dessert. He asked Addie about herself—her schooling, where she hailed from, her family—as if he didn't know every single bit of it already. Of course, she had to answer. To play nice and pretend. What other choice did she have?

It made her stomach turn. How she would make it through the whole weekend was unthinkable.

Richard had lost no time disappearing into his study after dessert, so at least she hadn't had to play any more make-believe. After cleaning up dinner and finishing the prep work for breakfast, Addie had walked by his study on her way upstairs. Through the glass French doors leading into the living room, she saw him in there alone, pouring what she suspected was one of multiple scotches he would consume before the night was out. If Richard noticed her pass by, he gave no indication.

She had no idea where Monica was, but wherever she was, she wasn't with Richard. It seemed that once dinner was over, they had gone their separate ways. Addie hadn't seen them together even once before dinner either. Despite Richard's claims, there was a distinct lack of evidence that he truly was working hard to fix his marriage.

Which made her decision easy.

Addie was too tired to leave tonight, but first thing in the morning she would text Sam. She would tell Monica she was feeling sick—which was one hundred percent true—and beg off after preparing breakfast. Addie would have to risk Monica getting angry enough over it to sabotage the restaurant.

If Monica does retaliate, surely her drive to hurt me won't last long.

It would definitely last less time than the rage that would ensue if Monica uncovered that Addie had dated her husband—something that could conceivably happen if Addie stuck around. At any moment, either Addie or Richard might unintentionally do something to give themselves away. Their proximity was one big truth bomb poised to explode.

I have to go. I'll call Sam in the morning and have him pick me up as early as possible.

All she had to do was get through the night.

12

ADDIE

Addie woke to the sound of breathing that wasn't her own. Her eyes snapped open, paralyzing fear invading her bones as she took in the dark figure hovering over her.

"Wha—"

"Shh," came a low voice, a hand reaching out to press two fingers against her mouth.

Addie shot up, sucking in a breath as her brain burst out of its sleep-addled stupor. "Richard! What are you doing?"

"I told you I'd explain."

Anger replaced the fear, straightening her spine. "You were supposed to do that hours ago. Hours!" Addie's voice was a rough whisper, urgent and annoyed. "Why did you leave me like that, serving you both...I just can't, Richard. Or Rob," she said, her voice curling around the false name he had given her.

He moved to sit on the edge of her bed and she shoved him

away. He huffed exasperatedly before kneeling beside it instead. He was far too close for her comfort. More than anything she wanted him to be as far away as possible. She had already made her decision. She didn't want to hear any explanation now. She didn't care what he had to say. The sight of him, swathed in the shadows of the night, was enough to upset her stomach. The scent of him didn't help either, a cocktail of pine and peat, likely the mixture of scotch on his breath and doses of aftershave, drumming up memories she didn't want taking up space in her head.

Please, please, go away.

"Look, it's the first chance I've had," Richard said. "She's been, I don't know, *around*. I never felt comfortable talking to you in the kitchen. I thought she might walk in."

"She? You mean *your wife?*"

"Yeah, Addie. My wife. The secret's out. I'm married. Yeah, I lied to you. All right? Satisfied? Are you going to let me explain or would you rather keep taking your pound of flesh?"

Addie heaved a disgusted sigh. "Fine." She gestured at him. "Explain."

"Thank you." He leaned in on his elbows, which brought him closer. Addie pulled back to compensate and keep a healthy distance between them. "As you've discovered, I have not been the perfect husband."

"Understatement of the century."

"Well, in my defense, Monica hasn't been the perfect wife."

"That isn't a defense."

He shrugged. "It's a reason. Anyway, after you made such a scene and bolted out of that restaurant—"

"Let me guess, you had a change of heart when I rejected you. You decided to turn over a new leaf and make your marriage work."

"No," he scoffed. "It's not like you were the...well..." he said, his words trailing off.

The Offer

"What…the first?" Addie asked, raising her eyebrows in mock surprise.

He nodded. "Exactly." He said it without the slightest hint of shame, which made Addie want to punch him. "So, you ending things wasn't a big deal, but *how* you left? That got to me. You made us a spectacle. I was embarrassed and angry. I charged out after you, ready to give you a piece of my mind. I saw you walking down the sidewalk across the street and ran after you. I wasn't paying attention. I stepped off the curb and was one second from being hit by a cab before some guy yanked me back. I could have been killed. Game over. *That* made me think. Made me reevaluate things. I realized I had to make some changes. Starting with my relationships. With my kids. And with Monica."

"Okay, good. Great. That's what you should be doing. But I don't see why that means I have to stay."

"Look, I've been killing myself to reshape my marriage since I last saw you. I've been at the office less, spending more time at home, and reaching out to my kids. It's working. If you leave now, after coming all the way here and with that much money at stake, Monica's going to be suspicious. She obviously remembers how much I enjoyed your restaurant. She knows I went multiple times. Monica will know something's up and make the connection. That can't happen, Addie. It'll ruin everything."

"Don't you think she's entitled to the truth?"

"I don't think that's your decision to make. Do you want to be responsible for blowing up what's left of my marriage just when I'm starting to make it work?"

"I wouldn't be the one blowing it up. That's all you."

"I might have created the bomb, but you'd be the one lighting the fuse."

Addie stared at him, trying to digest his take on all of it. She resented his lame attempt to lay any blame at her feet for whatever happened next. To make any of it her responsibility. But one thing he said did give her pause. She believed Monica had the right to know the truth about Richard, but was it Addie's place to tell her? Would she be overstepping if she left, knowing it would set destructive forces in motion?

It was a question she couldn't answer. The one thing she did know was she didn't want to be involved in this drama any more than she already was. Plus, there was a freckle-faced nine-year-old to think of. As hard as the idea was to accept, staying might be the least complicated option under the circumstances.

"Fine. I'll stay. I'll do the job," she said, hearing the dread in her voice. When a satisfied smile stretched across Richard's face, she added, "But I won't lie for you."

"You won't have to. You've made the right decision. Thank you."

"I'm not doing it for you," she whispered harshly.

"I don't care why you're doing it. I'm just glad you are." He pushed up off the floor and quietly stepped to the door, turning toward her as he reached it. "And think," he said, one eyebrow lifted, "you'll be ten thousand dollars richer when you get back to the city. I know you can use it."

Addie's mouth dropped at his audacity, but he didn't see her, having already stepped into the hall, the door closing behind him with a soft click.

After Richard left, Addie lay in bed for at least twenty minutes, breathing deeply and trying to fall back asleep. His words ran round and round in her head and made nodding off impossible. With a grunt, she sat up and checked the time with a groan.

Two in the morning.

Still far too early to go downstairs and start working on break-

The Offer

fast. Addie yawned, her gaze falling on her laptop. She always felt a little silly carrying both with her on trips, but she liked to use her iPad for cooking, especially with the touch-screen, and her laptop for research and everything else. Dragging them both everywhere was inconvenient, but that was how it was.

She turned on the small lamp on the nightstand and eyed the laptop. She could answer some emails, check her social media—but if she did that, she would never go back to sleep. In her experience, going online was the worst thing for insomnia. She needed sleep if she was going to deal with Richard being in the same house as she was. Instead, she got out of bed and walked to the large window overlooking the front of the property.

The moon, only a thin sliver, cast a nominal glow, enough to make out where the land met the river, and the gentle rippling of the water, the crests reflecting the meager light back at her. Something to the left caught her eye.

Monica was walking along the edge of the property at the shoreline. She seemed to be headed back to the house, though still a good thirty to forty yards away.

What is she doing out in the middle of the night like this?
Is she having trouble sleeping too?

But, hadn't Richard said Monica was asleep? If he was wrong about that, if he didn't know where she was, or if he was lying about it, what did that mean?

Maybe he and Monica aren't on as good of terms as he wants me to believe.

It was impossible to discern Monica's state of mind from her movements, and far too dark to get a good look at her expression. If she was angry, it wasn't ascertainable from the third-story window. Addie squinted. Had Monica looked up?

Addie stepped back, then looked at the lamp on the nightstand.

Uh-oh. The last thing she wanted was Monica thinking she was watching her. She clicked the light off and crawled back in bed. Maybe Monica hadn't seen her. She wouldn't bring it up if Monica didn't. No need to make things more awkward. As if that were possible.

Despite the unnerving effect of what had just transpired, Addie yawned.

A good sign.

She had a lot of work to do the next day and if she was going to stay, she would need to do it well. Addie prayed for her mind to quiet, peace to take hold, and sleep to come quickly.

They did.

13

NOT ADDIE

Adelaide Nichols was asleep, the covers rising and falling with every unhurried breath. Her dark brown hair a striking contrast against the stark-white pillowcases. One arm was up by her head, her hand resting open as if inviting the viewing.

If she only knew.

Despite the awkwardness, she stayed. And that's good. Really, really good.

It's the only way this will work. The clock's ticking down.

Finally.

More tapping on the keyboard pulled up video feeds from the other cameras, each opening in its own little square on the screen.

Maybe it's overkill, but nothing's going to be left to chance.

Nothing.

Because everything depends on getting this right.

14

ADDIE

The house was quiet when Addie rolled out of bed at five thirty in the morning, excruciatingly earlier than she was used to since her restaurant didn't serve breakfast and she didn't have to get to work until mid-afternoon. However, this weekend she was responsible for all meals, including breakfast, and in-between snacks. She had prepped a good bit yesterday afternoon, but there was still much left to do.

First things first, though.

Her bones complained a bit and a tingle behind her eyes suggested a headache might be coming on, both likely due to the fitful sleep she had endured. A shower worked out the kinks, though, and after dressing and throwing her hair into a messy bun, she pulled her Bible from her carry-all. It had been her grandmother's. The burgundy leather was worn, the pages filled with notes in the margins her Nana had scribbled over decades. The book was one of Addie's most cherished treasures.

A love of cooking wasn't the only thing her grandmother had instilled in her. Nana was the one who had first introduced Addie to Bible studies in the little sunroom of her coastal Maine home when Addie was only seven. Back then softbound books imparted the most basic of Bible stories, with simple words and pictures for Addie to color. Now she opened the study guide she was using to work her way through the Psalms one by one. The comprehensive and detailed work asked her to analyze each verse—each word—in light of the original Hebrew words and to record their meaning and her thoughts. She relished this type of in-depth study. It brought the verses to life in new ways.

After spending thirty minutes dissecting Psalm 46, a little less time than she would have generally dedicated to the endeavor because of the work awaiting her, she finished getting ready, applying a bit of makeup and twisting her long hair into a smooth low bun. She paused, taking stock of herself in the mirror. The woman staring back at her had come so far. It started when she was a teenage girl who drove thirty minutes from her middle-of-nowhere Maine town to Bar Harbor, to work in the kitchen of an upscale restaurant to gain experience. Now she was commanding ten thousand dollars for four days of work.

Not that this kind of windfall happens every day. Or that it'll ever happen again.

Even here she was doing work she loved. The work she had always wanted to do. That was a gift. If she was going to see this weekend through, it was time she started seeing the upsides. The silver linings. Find the blessings in the struggle. They certainly were there to be found, as long as she was willing to look. Grateful for the change in mindset, she headed downstairs.

No one was up and about. She padded in her tennis shoes to the kitchen, the ticking of the sleek, silver clock on the mantel the only other sound. After brewing a pot of French-pressed coffee, she put her earbuds in, hit play on her favorite "Mellow Morning Strings" playlist on Spotify, and started on breakfast. By the time she was done putting a batch of homemade cinnamon rolls in the oven, her mug was empty and she brewed what was bound to be the first of many pots of tea over the course of the day.

While the rolls baked, Addie looked over the weekend's menu again, getting her plan straight in her head. Soon the sweet vanilla and spice scent of the pastries rolled over the room. When Addie checked them, she found them cooked to pull-apart perfection. As she set the pan on the stove, her phone buzzed with a text from Monica.

> Hey. Could you bring up some coffee?
>
> Second floor, hallway to the right, third door on the left. You're a doll.

No, "Good morning." Just right to business. And—doll?

The term ruffled Addie's insides, but only because something about the way Monica had used it was terribly condescending. On top of that, Addie was a professional, hired for a specific job, which didn't include providing room service. The problem wasn't that Addie was above doing it. The problem was Monica was taking advantage.

On the other hand, with no housekeeper here this weekend I guess it makes sense. And I am being paid ten thousand dollars.

Despite Monica's diva-esque attitude pouring through the

The Offer

phone thicker than the icing on the cinnamon rolls, Addie supposed it wasn't too much to ask.

Her attitude in check, she loaded up a tray and made her way through the house with rolls, mugs of coffee, sugar, sweeteners and cream until reaching what she hoped was the right room. Addie knocked on the door and Monica swung it open so fast, Addie rocked back, splashing a little coffee onto the tray.

Monica's eyes brightened at the sight of her, and she swiped one of the mugs, downing a gulp as she held one finger up. "Ah, I needed this. Thanks." She turned her back on Addie but waved a hand for her to follow her inside, pointing at a side table. Addie set the tray down.

"I wasn't sure how you and Mr. Farrow take your coffee so I brought everything." The well-appointed room was overflowing with white—white linens, white curtains, white walls, white side chairs—all very modern—with more of that awful art on the walls. Monica had gotten her hands on this room too, no question.

"Is he ready for coffee?" Addie asked. "If not, I can make a fresh pot later—"

"I have no idea," Monica snipped. "We haven't shared a room for months. Sleep apnea, you know? He has the most horrible snoring. Was waking me up at all hours." She took another swig of coffee. "He took a room on the other side of the house," she said, giving a sharp tilt of her head. "But don't bother him. He'll come down for coffee when he wants it."

"Oh, okay," Addie said, moving toward the door. "I brought a few of my homemade cinnamon rolls with my secret recipe icing if you're hungry before breakfast—"

Monica glared at her like Addie had suggested she eat snakes. "I don't do carbs before my workout. Ever." She patted her non-existent belly. "I try to stay figure-conscious. I don't have the excuse for eating that your job gives you," she said, her eyes drifting to Addie's midsection.

The words might as well have been a wasp stinging Addie right between the eyes. Monica was clearly referencing the fluff at Addie's waistline. Of course there was fluff! So what? She was a chef. She loved food. One of her mottoes was, life is short, eat the good food. So she would be downing an entire cinnamon roll the minute she got back downstairs and be proud of it.

She sucked in the annoyed exhale threatening to escape and forced her smile wider. "In that case, I'll leave the coffee, but take the rolls," Addie said, reaching for the tray.

Monica nodded. "I can promise you Richard will want them," she said, rolling her eyes. "Today's his actual birthday, so I guess cake's appropriate. Or...something cake-like, right? Speaking of which, since it is his birthday, I'd like the special meal and dessert we spoke about served tonight. You saw that in the instructions?"

"Yes. I'll have it ready at seven thirty as requested."

"What about breakfast?" Monica asked, checking her watch before looking back at Addie. She had been specific about her daily egg-white and spinach omelet, grapefruit juice, and kale smoothie.

"Ready in twenty minutes." Addie had prepped everything the night before, which made the morning meal quick and easy.

"Perfect. I'll have it on the back terrace." She turned her back on Addie, sashaying toward the bathroom, raising and wiggling the fingers of one hand in a blind dismissal. "Close the door on your way out."

Addie carried the tray back downstairs, finally allowing the exhale to escape in a long hiss of air. How anyone worked for Monica on a regular basis, she couldn't fathom. Monica left no doubt she considered "the help" to be second-class citizens.

If this is what I have to deal with, I can't imagine what the poor housekeeper must endure.

The Offer

Once back in the kitchen, she set the tray on the counter a bit harder than she intended, causing the plate and remaining mug to clink together and more coffee to splash out. Addie turned, reaching for a paper towel, and through the front-facing windows saw dark clouds gathering, promising rain. Movement down by the pier caught her eye and she leaned closer to the glass.

Sam was back. And someone was with him.

15

ADDIE

"What's he doing here?"

Addie spun to find Richard, dressed in jeans and an MIT sweatshirt, standing right behind her.

Too close. Much, much too close.

Addie slid several paces away. "Sorry, I didn't know you were up. Can I get—"

"And why is Tanya with him?" his baritone boomed, a hint of red peeking from his collar as he stared at Sam and the woman following him up the walk. "I thought Monica said she wasn't coming. She was keeping this small. No kids, no help."

Addie's chest tightened, disgust welling up inside her. The aggravation in Richard's tone underscored how profoundly he hadn't wanted anyone at the cottage that weekend, *including his children*. Would he have been just as annoyed if they had turned up,

The Offer

instead of the housekeeper? Addie couldn't help but question once again what kind of father Richard had been.

If it's anything like the kind of husband he's been, then not a good one.

"Ugh," he grunted, taking one last look outside before snapping his gaze to Addie. "Did Monica say anything to you?"

Addie shook her head. "No. I don't know anything about it. All I know is there's coffee and cinnamon rolls, and I'm making custom omelets." She gestured at a sheet of paper on the kitchen island. "A list of available ingredients is on the menu—"

Without waiting for her to finish, Richard stepped to the island to peruse the list. After scanning it, he looked at her pointedly. Without anything in his gaze or tone to suggest she was anything more than hired help, he rattled off what he wanted, ending with an unenthusiastic, "I'll be downstairs. In the media room. Bring it down when it's ready." His attitude was dismissive and cold and a farce, as if he hadn't snuck into her bedroom in the middle of the night to beg for her help.

She wasn't having it.

Addie might have to endure that kind of behavior from Monica, but no way was she taking it from Richard. Not when she was the one doing *him* a favor by staying. She wasn't going to let him pretend they both didn't know what was going on.

She took a step back, cocked her head, and arched her eyebrows defiantly.

"Oh, right," he said, taking the hint. His sharp tone adopted a conciliatory note. "Sorry. Forgot who I was talking to. Force of habit."

"I'll bet. You talk to your employees like that? I'm surprised you have any left."

"We pay well. Which," he paused, a faint smirk pulling on the corner of his mouth, "you already know. People tend to put up with a lot for the right kind of money. Say, for instance...when their restaurant needs a cash boost..."

She *hated* that he knew that. He had seen her apartment. He knew how she lived. She had even talked about the restaurant's struggles. Now he was throwing it in her face. Lording it over her.

"Maybe I should go," she snapped, red-hot anger simmering in her soul, coloring her thinking. It wasn't her responsibility to keep Richard's mess from coming to light. So why should she go out of her way to help him if he was going to subject her to this kind of treatment all weekend? "Sam's here now. He can take me back."

Addie started to turn and Richard grasped her arm. She wrenched it from him, and he clasped his hands together and sighed.

"Look, I'm sorry," he said in a forced, pleading voice that didn't match the hard look in his eyes. "I'm only messing with you. Please stay. You have to. I promise I'll behave."

Addie didn't believe him. Not in the slightest.

She took a breath, trying to calm down. Trying to make a decision not based on anger, disgust, or...dare she admit it...payback. When she thought about it rationally, only one decision made sense under the circumstances. Addie nodded her assent, desperately hoping she wouldn't regret it.

Once he left her in peace, Addie whipped up the personalized breakfasts for the Farrows and delivered their respective trays to them in their separate locations. These two spent hardly any time together at all. It was hard to imagine living with someone and making so much effort to avoid being near them in your own home. But given Richard's proclivities, it made sense. Though if he wanted

The Offer

to smooth things out, spending time with his wife would be a good way to start.

After promising both she would return to collect the trays in a little while, she headed back to the kitchen to clean up and start working on the rest of the day's offerings. Her fingers were working the dough for the tomato-basil-mozzarella bruschetta she was going to serve as part of an afternoon charcuterie board, when a glance out the window revealed Sam standing on the Farrows' boat.

Addie turned, looked back at the full plate of cinnamon rolls by the stove, and made a decision.

"Hello?"

Addie stood on the dock beside the Farrows' enormous boat. Nearly twice the size of Sam's craft, it had two levels above the waterline and a sundeck at the stern. Sam had been standing on the deck when she started down the walk, but now he was gone.

"Sam? Are you still here?"

She waited several moments, then called out again. This time footsteps emanated from the center of the boat, growing louder until Sam walked through a doorway from the internal cabin onto the foredeck.

"Sorry about that," he said, running a hand through his hair, smoothing it down. Today he wore a black T-shirt and jeans. "I was in the engine room below deck."

"So it's not only your brother who works on boats?" Addie asked.

"I do anything that's needed. We didn't have a time slot for taking a look at this until next week, but then it dawned on me I could at least take a look while I was dropping Tanya off. See if I need to order any parts." He wiped a hand across his forehead, leaving a black streak. "Good thing I did, 'cause it's a mess. Some kind of electrical short."

Addie gestured toward the mark on his forehead. "Um, you've got..." She drew an imaginary line on her forehead. He glanced down at his hands, spotted with what Addie presumed to be oil or grease. He pulled a cloth from his back pocket, cleaned his hands, then did the same to his forehead. "Did I get it?"

"Yep. All good."

He shoved the cloth back into his pocket, eyeing the plate in her hands. "Whatcha got there?"

Addie held the plate of pastries out to him. "I brought this down for you. We had extra. Didn't want them to go to waste."

Sam's mouth split in a boyish grin. "Now we're talking." He closed the distance as she held the plate in one hand and the railing with the other, and stepped over the side and down onto the boat deck. "Hey, be careful," he cautioned, hurrying over and reaching her right as she planted both feet. "That first step can be shaky. I would've helped."

"No worries. I'm good, thanks." She held the plate out and he grinned again, snatching a cinnamon bun, then leaning against the cockpit.

"Mrs. Farrow didn't mind you bringing these down?" he asked, taking a bite, then wiping icing from his upper lip. "Wow, they're really good."

"Thanks. And Mrs. Farrow doesn't know. I don't think she would care. She didn't want them."

"Figures. Me, I've got a weakness for anything sweet and baked. Nearly got into a fight once over the last piece of cake."

"Must've been good cake."

"It was chocolate. Need I say more?" He inhaled another bite. "I've always suspected Mrs. Farrow's more the 'only-salads-with-no-dressing' type." He winked. "You know, always hungry, always grumpy."

Addie let an amused snort slip. "I thought you said talking about your clients wasn't a good idea."

"Well," he said, pulling off another strip of doughy goodness, "you brought me cinnamon rolls. Makes you trustworthy in my book."

"You know," she started, still weighing whether she should share, when the rest tumbled out, "I almost texted you last night for a ride back. This is…turning out to be a little harder than I thought it would be."

"Oh, yeah?" Sam said, cocking his head. "Working for the Farrows isn't quite what you were expecting?"

Addie clicked her tongue. "You might say that."

"Hmm. Can't say I'm surprised." He took another bite. "But you're still here." He held up what was left of the roll. "And cooking. I'm assuming you decided to stay?"

"I did."

"Why?"

Fair question. Just not one I'm going to answer. At least not fully.

"I said I would do the job, so I'm sticking it out. Though, I'll be glad to see you Monday afternoon."

At the comment he squinted, eyeing her carefully, his features contracting. Insecurity rippled through Addie, as it was a bit like being x-rayed. She wondered if her expression was betraying more than she cared to. "Are you sure?" he asked, his voice a smidge softer. "I can take you back now if you want. You don't have to stick it out if they're making you miserable."

"No. Honestly, I'm fine. I'm a professional. I can deal with it."

He raised his eyebrows doubtfully. "If you say so." He finished off the cinnamon roll and rubbed his hands together to remove any lingering glaze and crumbs. "At least you get to stay in that house. What do you think of it?"

"It's...big."

He chuckled. "That's it?"

"I mean, it's gorgeous, of course. Mrs. Farrow gave me a quick tour. But I'm spending most of my time in the kitchen, which is amazing. The stove alone...it's the kind of kitchen I dream about owning one day."

"Did she take you to the fifth floor?" He pointed to the highest point of the house which rose above the tallest chimney, consisting of a large turret with two dormers, both facing the water.

"No. Haven't made it up there."

"It's just one room. A lookout of sorts. Has great views."

"You've been in it?"

He nodded. "The last owner showed it to me. From there you can see up and down the river as far as the eye allows. The story goes that the original builders were involved in the bootlegging trade and used it to keep an eye out for the authorities, rival bootleggers, and such—trouble in general. When I saw it, Mr. Crenshaw —he was the last owner—was using it as a library. It still had the original bookcases. He showed me that the bottom section in the middle had a hidden compartment. A little lever under the molding popped it right open. Wouldn't know it existed unless you already knew where to look for it. Mr. Crenshaw was so proud of it. Said he stumbled onto it while refinishing the wood himself. He used it as a safe and speculated the bootleggers used it to hide their product, cash or—" Sam tilted his head. "—would that have been gold back then? Anyway, they used it to hide whatever they didn't want found or confiscated." He donned a wistful expression. "It may not be there anymore. Given Mrs. Farrow's taste, she's probably had them ripped out by now. Would've been too old-fashioned looking."

"Ahh...so you've noticed her decor choices."

"The way she's made up the downstairs? Putting *that* stuff in *that* house. It should be a crime."

A smile curved Addie's mouth. "You're not wrong. The master bedroom's worse, by the way, if you haven't seen it."

"Ugh. I can imagine."

A few moments passed in silence. Addie shifted her weight for the lack of anything else to do, then said, "I'll check on the bookcases and when you come back, I'll let you know if they survived Monica Farrow."

"I hope she left well enough alone. The way Crenshaw had it fixed up with all those books and a couple of big chairs…add a good thunderstorm and it would be the perfect place to disappear in a novel."

"You're a reader?"

"It's pretty much my main pastime. At least once football season ends."

Loves books, easy to talk to, smart and runs his own business. I'm surprised a ring isn't on his finger.

The boat rocked and she suddenly realized her gaze might have lingered a bit too long on him. She uttered a hurried, "Me too—I'm a reader, I mean. Not as much into football. I'm more of a hockey fan."

"Huh. Too bad," Sam said, shrugging in exaggerated fashion. "Guess the wedding's off."

Addie chuckled. "Guess so." She looked up at the house. "So, is this one of the homes in the area with some good stories tied to it? One of the places the local tours talk about?"

"Yeah, but I think they mostly make vague remarks about bootleggers building and using the house and speculate about what might be buried on the island, stuff like that. Never anything specific like what Crenshaw showed me. If the tour operators don't already know about it, I won't be the one spilling the house's secrets.

The Farrows already complain about the tours getting too close to the island—shocking, right? I wouldn't want to be responsible for boats lingering with longer tales. Mr. Farrow wouldn't be happy about it and I've seen him unhappy. Don't want to be on the receiving end of that."

"You're not kidding. He wasn't happy when you turned up with their housekeeper this morning."

Sam's eyes narrowed, his forehead furrowing. "What? Why? I always bring Tanya out on Saturday mornings. They still have her come out on weekends when they aren't here. She needs steady employment and they don't want to lose her. Or at least that's what she tells me."

"Both of them led me to believe the housekeeper wouldn't be here this weekend. Told me I'd have to fill in for her. Mrs. Farrow said she decided to keep the staff to a minimum for privacy."

"Well, no one told me."

"She probably forgot, got lost in her handling all the other details for this weekend."

"Mmm." He glanced at the house. "I can take her back if they want. But I'd have to do it now. I'm supposed to be at another place, far south of here, for the rest of the day. I need to leave soon."

Addie also looked up at the house, curious if anyone was watching them. She didn't see any faces in windows, but that didn't mean anything. She turned back to Sam and shrugged. "Mr. Farrow saw you two coming off the boat and Tanya's already inside. If neither of them has reached out to you, I'm sure it's fine. The Farrows must have decided it would be nice to have the extra help. I'm not much of a waitress and I'm a horrible housekeeper. I'm sure they'll find plenty to keep her busy."

"You're probably right." He checked his watch. "I should head out. I've got that appointment to get to."

He held a hand out to Addie again and she took it, this time using it to steady herself as she stepped back onto the dock. It was stupid, but she liked the feel of his hand in hers. She couldn't remember the last time someone held her hand like that. Protectively. Intentionally. It had been long before Richard entered the picture, that was for sure.

"Thanks," she told him, pulling her hand back once her feet were planted on the dock.

"Thank you for the cinnamon roll."

She nodded, then started walking toward the path that would take her around the back of the house.

"Hey, um, Addie?"

She swiveled in his direction. "Yeah?"

"Uh, I wouldn't complain if you left the rest of those."

A smile tugging her lips, she loosely wrapped the other two rolls in one of the paper napkins she had brought and passed them over.

He took them from her and after hesitating, said, "Listen, if you change your mind about staying, if you end up wanting to leave, text me, okay? Or call or whatever. I'll come for you. Day or night. Middle of the night. Whenever."

Warmth spread through Addie's center as she registered an intensity in his gaze that made it clear he was genuinely concerned. This was the sort of thoughtful kindness she might have expected from friends and family, but not strangers. "Middle of the night? I couldn't ask you to do that. You're not a water taxi."

The corner of his mouth edged up. "That's kind of exactly what I am."

Heat flushed her cheeks and she chuckled. "Oh. Right. But not at all hours."

"For you, I'd make an exception. You're not stuck here, okay?"

"Okay. Thanks," she said, turning and leaving him to the boat as she walked back to the house.

No matter what happened with the Farrows, she wasn't going to put him out like that. He already said he had things to do. She wasn't adding to his workload. She was a big girl, and a professional, as she kept telling herself. She would be fine.

After all, she only had two days, three hours, and thirty-five minutes left to go.

16

ADDIE

"I'm not feeling well," Monica announced as she walked into the kitchen a few minutes before noon.

Addie jumped at the unexpected noise, then swiveled from the stove where she was searing scallops for the seafood pasta she was serving for lunch. "I'm sorry. Is there anything I can do?"

Monica waved a hand. "I'll be fine. My stomach's just a little off. I wanted to grab some ginger ale to settle it." She headed to the refrigerator and Addie refocused on the scallops. It would only take seconds for them to go from perfectly seared to burned. She turned them once and was so intent on monitoring their progress, that it wasn't until another minute went by that she realized Monica was still standing at the fridge. Alarm bells dinged in her head.

Addie swiveled around. Monica looked like Addie's four-year-old nephew when she caught him in the pantry eating straight out of a bag of sugar. A disingenuous sheepish smile parted Monica's lips. "Sooorrrry," she drawled, not sounding sorry at all. "I couldn't resist tasting the whipped cream. Did you make this from scratch?" she asked, licking her finger and pointing to the glass Irish coffee mugs filled with alternating layers of sea-salt-caramel-coffee mousse and whipped cream. A final dollop of cream sprinkled with chocolate shavings topped each one.

The dollop Monica had just violated on the mug nearest her.

"I did," Addie answered, working hard to hide her annoyance. No chef likes their food to be tampered with.

"And you made four?" Monica asked.

"There's two of you and I made two extra ones, just in case."

"Well, if you wouldn't mind—and I know this sounds awful—but I'm sure sometimes you, you know, sample the leftovers. And, well…" Her eyes flitted up and down Addie. "…you chefs tend to like your sweets. Ordinarily, I wouldn't care, but would you leave those for Richard? I'm positive he'll want seconds and thirds over the weekend. I mean, it is his birthday." She closed the fridge, ginger ale in hand, and slinked over to a cabinet where she retrieved a glass.

"Of course," Addie said, remaining professional and composed on the outside while fuming on the inside.

"I know you like your sweets?" What's that supposed to mean? The nerve of this woman.

"Thanks, hon," Monica said, pouring the soda into the glass, and giving a quick shrug and saccharin smile before waltzing toward the living room. She was nearly through the doorway when she stopped. "Oh," she said, turning back to Addie. "One other thing. You did fine with the service last night, but," Monica winced theatrically, "you let a little too much time go between courses. Again, I'm sorry the housekeeper isn't here to handle it. I know you hadn't planned on waiting on us, but if you would adjust that one tiny thing…okay?"

"But," Addie said, "she *is* here."

The Offer

"Who?"

"Your housekeeper. Tanya? Sam—the boat guy—dropped her off this morning."

A shadow crossed Monica's face. "What?"

"Sam brought her here this morning." Monica continued to stare at her like she was speaking another language. "Rich—Mr. Farrow saw her. Saw them when they arrived. He didn't tell you?"

Monica's lips pursed, her eyebrows furrowing so deeply that it threatened to undo everything the Botox had achieved. She stepped to the island and forcefully plopped her glass onto the granite, leaving Addie surprised it hadn't shattered.

"I haven't seen Richard all day," Monica said, her voice notably lower-pitched. "He's doing his thing and I'm—it doesn't matter. Where is Tanya now?"

Addie shrugged. "No idea. She passed through a few times. Said something about cleaning rooms upstairs?" The first time Tanya came through the kitchen, Addie had introduced herself and tried to strike up a conversation. Beyond getting the straight facts—her name and that she was a student at Jefferson Community College in nearby Watertown—the woman hadn't been interested in interacting. Hadn't said a word the other times she walked through. "She said she had a lot of house to cover in two days."

Monica groaned, throwing her head back. "I didn't want her here. I wanted this weekend to be a simple, intimate event." She huffed. "How did I forget about her? I could have sworn I told her I didn't need her this weekend."

"Maybe you did tell her and she forgot," Addie offered generously.

"Doesn't matter. I'll handle it. I will need you to please make sure dinner's ready on time, all right?" she snapped, before spinning on her heel and striding out.

At least she said please.

As she watched Monica go, Addie's heart went out to Tanya. The poor woman was probably about to be on the receiving end of a very unpleasant conversation.

Fifteen minutes later, Monica returned, informing Addie she had banished Tanya to the guest cottage. "It's been needing to be cleaned out for ages, anyway. She'll leave tomorrow night at the normal time. So we're back to the original plan. You'll be serving tonight."

Addie nodded. "Understood. Not a problem."

"Good." Monica swept her previously abandoned glass of ginger ale off the island and raised it in a mock toast. "Here's to no more hiccups."

17

NOT ADDIE

Most people think the best part of a show is the ending when the plot all comes together.

It's not.

Not that a satisfying ending isn't a good thing. It is. But it isn't the best part.

The most intoxicating part of a show is the moment right before the curtain goes up.

That instant when the house lights go down and a hush falls over the crowd. The suspense is electric. You can feel it throbbing through the room, poised on a pin, waiting to tip.

There's nothing quite like it. Knowing the audience is on the edge of their seats, breathless and silent, eyes and ears trained laser-like on center stage. Because they know something good is coming. That only ticking seconds on the clock stand between them and what they've been waiting for.

That's what it's like for me now. Heart racing. Pulse pounding.
The show's about to start.
And I've got a front-row seat.

18

ADDIE

The storm that had been threatening to let loose all day finally raged outside as Addie worked to put the finishing touches on dinner. Against the steady drumming of pounding rain and flashing lightning, she had already served hors d'oeuvres in the living room, where Monica and Richard seemed to be having the first quality time they had shared since Addie arrived. All through dinner the night before it had been painfully quiet, in an atmosphere so cold Addie could have sworn someone had ratcheted the thermostat down as far as it would go. But tonight she had found them sitting on the couch together, smiling, even chuckling. When Monica asked Addie for her pre-dinner gimlet, Richard stood, volunteering to retrieve it along with his martini.

Maybe it's softened them up, it being his birthday and all. Maybe Richard truly is trying to make amends and repair his marriage.

This wasn't enough to keep a prickly discomfort from snaking up her spine as Richard followed her back to the kitchen. She didn't want to be alone with him. She wasn't sure what he might say or do. To her surprise, he had simply waited patiently, making a few brief comments about the storm while Addie prepared the drinks. When she finished, he carried them back to Monica without so much as an awkward glance at Addie.

Twenty minutes later, Addie had informed them that dinner was ready, but instead of them heading to the dining room, Richard followed her to the kitchen again, announcing they wanted a second round of drinks first. As he didn't want anything to be ruined, cold, or burned because Addie was distracted with making them—as if she would let that happen—he set about preparing the cocktails himself. Addie's internal danger sensor ramped up again as he worked, the space in the kitchen seeming to shrink around them.

Is he trying to test me? See what I'll say? Oh please don't let it be that he wants to be close to me.

The last idea had turned her stomach, but again to her relief, Richard did nothing untoward. He made the drinks and left. Now Addie leaned against the counter, taking a sip from the last cup of tea left in the pot, enjoying a momentary calm before dinner began. The day had already been a long one. Though less work than she was used to, it was more emotionally taxing. The fatigue that usually hit her around midnight on a workday was claiming her early. Even her bones were tired, occasional achy jabs firing in her shins from the standing. She brought the teacup up, relishing the steadying scent of bergamot in the Earl Grey that always settled her soul. After draining the last dregs, she set the cup down and patted the counter.

"All right, then. Showtime."

Addie decided to preemptively fill the glasses and wine goblets, hoping the sound would carry and encourage Monica and Richard

The Offer

to come in. If they waited too much longer, the timing would be off and dinner would suffer. She pushed through the swinging door leading to the dining room where a large, contemporary-style ebony table surrounded by white leather chairs was set with candles and fine china. Crystal goblets sparkled in the flickering light, making shadows dance on the low centerpiece of white silk roses. The only color in the room, once again, was an unframed canvas splashed with a variety of red hues in no discernible pattern.

Addie started pouring the wine, ruing the merlot Monica had insisted upon. A white would have been a better complement to the first two courses, but Monica was insistent they didn't like white wine, though Addie had seen Richard drink it on more than one occasion. She suspected Monica was the one who preferred the red.

Footsteps sounded from the main hall and Addie turned to see the couple walking in.

"Oh, how charming!" Monica declared as Richard pulled her chair out for her—an uncharacteristic act of chivalry Addie suspected, given the look on Monica's face. Monica set down her half-finished second gimlet, exchanging it for the wine goblet. She swirled it beneath her nose to sample the wine's bouquet as Richard took his seat.

Addie stepped back to address them, taking a deep breath and praying she could make it through without rolling her eyes. "Mr. Farrow, happy birthday. I hope you enjoy dinner. It's been carefully crafted for you based on Mrs. Farrow's detailed recommendations. Please let me know if you have any questions, or if I can do anything to make the experience better."

While Monica stared adoringly at Richard—something was undeniably artificial and forced about it—he plopped his hands on the table, rattling the silverware. "Thank you for the birthday wishes, Addie. I can't wait to eat. I know your food never disappoints."

Ugh.

Every word out of his mouth fell on her ears like nails on a chalkboard. Still, Addie managed to push the disgust down, nod, and offer what she hoped was a grateful smile at his compliment. "Well, let's get started, then, shall we? I'll be right back with the first course."

Addie pushed through to the kitchen, sighing heavily once she was out of earshot. If the cordiality between the couple didn't feel so contrived, she would have been glad to see them relating more positively to each other because, up to this point, there had been no evidence of a real relationship of any kind. This sad coexistence the Farrows maintained was pitiable. Especially knowing what she knew about Richard's extracurricular activities. She already knew it wasn't a model marriage, but if the last thirty hours were anything to go by, it wasn't even a friendship.

If pressed, the best thing she could say to describe them would be, indifferent. Quite the opposite of the enamored wife Monica had portrayed herself to be when she showed up at the restaurant two nights ago. Or the reformed husband desperate to repair a broken marriage who Richard claimed to be last night.

Addie yawned. She blinked and shook it off, willing herself into a state of mental alertness. She wasn't sure whether the yawn was prompted by tiredness or her tendency to use sleep as an escape mechanism—not surprising given how much she would love to escape her current situation. Either way, she had a long way to go before her head would hit a pillow.

"Pull it together, Chef," she mumbled. "You can sleep when dinner's done."

Addie's mind drifted as she put the final touches on the appetizer course.

Why would Monica go to so much trouble for Richard when so far, their behavior indicates no love is lost between them?

The Offer

Was she just keeping up appearances? If so, for whom? Richard? The outside world? Did she just want to be able to tell her friends she had lured a chef from one of Manhattan's up-and-coming restaurants to be their private caterer for Richard's birthday? Was she working that hard to keep up the image of the dutiful, loving wife? Was it all fake?

Addie hoped not. Whatever had happened between her and Richard, Addie did want him to pull his marriage together, if for nothing more than the sake of his young child. But if this was as good as it got between Richard and Monica, it was a pretty sad state of affairs. Certainly not how she wanted her marriage to be, whenever the time came. She wanted a marriage like her parents had. Solid. Dear. Lasting. On her parents' thirty-fifth anniversary, Addie overheard her father tell her mother that he was still so in love with her. That was what Addie wanted. It was the only thing she would accept. Anything else was settling.

For the second time since the storm began, the lights flickered. And for the second time, Addie was grateful the kitchen was outfitted with a gas stove. Loss of power would have made preparation difficult, if not impossible, otherwise. She yawned again before realizing what she was doing, then rolled her neck and shook her head to get the cobwebs out. She snatched up both plates of pear-and-almond pastries paired with a fruit salad with honey-mint glaze, and carried them into the dining room.

"Beautiful," Monica remarked, as Addie set the first plate in front of her.

"This looks incredible!" Richard gushed, when she moved to him. "Really, Chef, you've outdone yourself."

The compliments twisted in Addie's belly. Why couldn't he just take the plate and stuff his mouth in silence?

"Thanks. Enjoy," she droned, aware that she sounded less than enthusiastic, but not caring enough to try harder. She quickly slipped through the door, hoping to get back to the kitchen before any more overdone compliments came her way.

One of the primary goals of a chef is to properly pace the meal. Not too slow and not too fast. In this case, Addie would have been happy to get the whole thing over with in thirty minutes. Nevertheless, she was a professional. If she was going to do this, she was going to do it right.

She took her time plating the salad course—pickled green tomatoes topped with goat cheese, bacon, and a creamy balsamic vinegar dressing—and washed some of the dishes, reducing the work that would be necessary as part of the post-dinner cleanup. When sufficient time had passed for them to have finished the appetizers, Addie gathered the salad plates and started for the dining room. "I hope you enjoy this," she announced, swapping out Monica's plates first. "It's a specialty of mine, along with the dessert this evening."

Monica looked up from the salad plate to Richard, her teeth gleaming beacons in an impetuous smile. "That'll be the caramel thingy you're so fond of from Addie's restaurant." She winked at him and downed the last of her martini.

Richard's eyes lit up. "Really?"

"Yes. Mrs. Farrow requested it specifically," Addie replied, now exchanging Richard's plates.

"I do love that dessert," he said, and gave Monica a little tilt of his head. "Thank you, babe."

Babe? Ugh.

The pretense, because it plainly came off like pretense, made Addie sick to her stomach again. Addie's free hand drifted to her belly to quell the wave of nausea. She stepped toward the kitchen, determined to exit before having to listen to any more.

"I wanted to give you the birthday you deserve," Monica said, pausing to inhale a sharp breath. "You've been working so hard lately. I—" She cut herself off, sucking in another breath before letting out a panicked squeak.

The sound halted Addie in her steps. She twisted back toward the table so fast that it threw her off balance. She righted herself as she locked eyes with Monica. "Monica?"

"I..." Monica tried again, unable to finish her thought, her eyes wide. Something wasn't right. Monica's face was now deathly white, beads of moisture dotting her forehead.

"Monica? What's wrong?"

Monica wiped a hand across her forehead, then put her palm to her cheek. "I'm...fine." She lifted her wine glass to her lips and sipped. Leaning back, she set the glass down and fanned herself with her napkin. "I'm just hot all of a sudden."

"Maybe you should stop drinking," Richard said sardonically, his words devoid of compassion.

"Maybe you should mind your own business," Monica answered, but her voice was weak and her tone lacked bite. She sucked in another breath, her hand going to her chest. "I'm...my heart's racing." She closed her eyes, her face distorting, her breaths coming ragged and quick. "I can't catch...my—"

Monica slid out of her chair.

"Monica!" Addie yelled, racing to her side and catching her by the arm in time to keep her from hitting the floor.

Richard shoved his chair back and stood, the grating sound ripping through the room. "Monica?" Addie asked again.

"I...can't," Monica managed to eke out as Addie squatted, lowering her to the floor. Addie pulled off her apron and balled it up, placing it beneath Monica's head.

"Monica, it's going to be okay."

Monica's every breath was a struggle, labored wheezing ending in a tight, sucking sound. Her features were seized in pain, terror flooding her gaze. "Help..." she said weakly.

Addie spun to Richard, expecting him to be right behind her, calling 9-1-1. He wasn't. He stood motionless by his chair, his eyes trained on his struggling wife.

"Richard!" Addie yelled. "Help her! Do something!"

His gaze shifted from Monica to Addie, his countenance stony. He still didn't move.

"Richard!" Addie yelled again, then forgot him as pained gasps drew her attention back to Monica, whose eyes were losing focus. Addie grabbed Monica's shoulders. "Monica! Stay with me!"

Monica shuddered, gave one last gasp, then grew still.

19

ADDIE

Addie knelt over Monica, shaking her without effect. "Monica! Monica!" she begged, her voice quivering. When Monica didn't move, Addie sat back up and reached into her pocket for her phone.

It wasn't there. She had left it in the kitchen.

"Richard!" she yelled, turning toward him. Disbelief washed over her. He was still in the same position, his expression blank. "Call 9-1-1!"

But he didn't reach for his phone. "It's too late," he murmured, at last moving to stand beside Addie, looking down on his wife. "She's dead."

"You don't know that!" She grabbed Monica's wrist, pulling it toward her and searching for a pulse. Even as she did, one look at Monica's glassy stare told her she wouldn't find one.

Richard was right. Monica was dead.

A cry threatened to erupt in Addie's throat, but she choked it back. With shaking fingers, she gently laid Monica's hand back on her chest and swiveled to Richard. "Why didn't you do something? You could have tried. You could have called 9-1-1. Does she have a heart condition? What medication is she on?" Then another horror occurred to her and her stomach plummeted.

An allergy! Does she have an allergy she forgot to tell me about?

"Does she have an allergy?" Addie bellowed at the comatose Richard. "She does, doesn't she? Why didn't she tell me?" He didn't reply. "Richard," she pressed, "I need you to answer me."

No tears filled his eyes. No concern was etched into the lines of his face. He straightened, dropped his shoulders, and spoke evenly. "Addie," he said, cocking his head slowly, "What have you done?"

The bottom dropped out of Addie's world. "What...what do you mean, what have I done?"

"You've killed her." His face was hard and his eyes, dark.

"I..." Addie rocketed up and stepped back from him. The room tilted and she grabbed onto the table for support. "I...she didn't tell me she had an allergy...I didn't..."

"Was this your plan once you realized Monica had hired you? When you realized who she was? Get rid of Monica—the reason we couldn't be together?" His words were cold and calculated, though nothing he was saying made sense.

"What? That's ridiculous. Stop it, Richard, and call 9-1-1. She could still be..."

"She isn't anything. You made sure of that." He stepped around Addie, over the body of his wife without sparing her a look, and stopped behind Monica's chair. Addie followed his gaze to Monica's martini glass. He gestured to it but said nothing.

The shock addled his brain. He's not thinking straight.

If help was going to be called, Addie was going to have to do it. She started for the door to the kitchen, intending to get her phone, but Richard caught her arm and yanked her back. She nearly tripped on Monica, stumbling over her own feet to avoid trampling on the body, causing her to fall into Richard. He caught her and spun her so Monica's martini glass was in her eyeline.

"You did this. You knew about her antidepressant meds. I told you about them while we were dating. You were one of the reasons she was on them. Because of us."

"No, you didn't. You never told me you were married at all! Wait—so she doesn't have an allergy?"

"Of course not," he said, and though she should have been relieved this wasn't her fault, something about the growing smirk on his face terrified her.

"So what—"

"You made this drink for her."

"No, I didn't. You did."

"No, honey. *You* did."

Addie's gaze took in the glass, then the body on the floor, then the ever so slight bit of liquid pooling in the bottom of the glass. The little bit Monica hadn't drained.

Noooo...

The stoic look on Richard's face. His failure to call 9-1-1. The bizarre things he was saying that weren't true.

He couldn't have...

"You knew exactly who she was when she hired you," he said calmly. "You concocted this scheme to get her out of the way. Overdose her on her own antidepressants and bring on a heart attack—"

"I didn't even know she existed, much less that she was on medication—"

"Sure you did. Because I told you about her clontriptyline while we were going out. You crushed them up and laced her drink. The drink she has at least once or more *every* night. You figured once she was out of the way, you would be able to convince me to take you back. Then we would stage her upstairs, tell the authorities she took the news about me leaving her badly and went off and killed herself by overdose. You were pretty disappointed when I *didn't* go along with your plan and instead called the police."

Addie's pulse thundered in her head. "What are you talking about? Nothing you're saying is true! I didn't make that drink. *You* did. And you know I don't know anything about her medication." She shook her arm, but his grip was like iron. "Let me go," she spat.

Panic was crushing her, making her weak, her legs threatening to give out any second. She couldn't allow that. She needed to be strong.

Get. It. Together.

"Let go, I said!" she yelled when he only held her tighter.

"I can't let go, Addie. I've got to keep you somewhere safe until the authorities arrive. Can't have you running off. You're my ex-mistress and you just murdered my wife."

"I wasn't your mistress and I did not murder your wife!"

"That's not what the police will believe. Not when they find your emails to me."

"What emails?" Addie was shouting now. "I didn't send you any emails!"

"Your server records will say otherwise. So sad. You couldn't handle my breaking up with you after I saw the error of my ways and how we were hurting Monica. I wanted to repair things with my wife." He spread his arms wide. "This weekend away, just the two of us, was part of that. But Monica unknowingly went and hired you. The woman who has been stalking me by email. The woman who won't let me go."

All feeling drained from Addie's body.

Somehow, he planned this. Without knowing I was coming.

That isn't possible, is it?

"I'm calling the police!" she cried and again worked to wrest his hand away. This time he let go. Angry red lines marked where his fingers had gripped her.

"Go ahead. If you don't, I will. They'll find everything I planted. Including the crushed pill residue in your bag."

Addie gasped. This was too much. Her spiraling brain couldn't make sense of it. He had set her up? Planted evidence? She swallowed hard.

Killed his wife.

But how? The pill residue he could easily manage, but the emails? He couldn't do that.

"There are no emails," she challenged.

A sinister smile twisted his lips. "You're smarter than this, Addie. It's one of the reasons I liked you." He paused, and when she didn't reply, said, "You know what I do for a living, right? I mean, you had to have registered it once you got here and I was the one who answered the door. I know I told you I was working in IT when we were dating, but..." He paused again for what felt like effect, and appeared amused.

He's enjoying this.

"I have to confess I wasn't completely truthful." He snorted. "I don't work in IT. I own the company and have my fingers in...a few other pies. I enlisted the help of a very talented hacker involved in one of my side gigs to put those emails together. They'll never trace it back. Trust me. We're good at what we do. It'll look like you sent every one of them, you poor, misguided, love-struck cast-off."

The inside of Addie's head was a tornado of emotion and disbelief. A woman was dead and she was being framed for it. She wanted to scream, to yell, to wake herself from this nightmare, but all she could produce was a whisper. "Why?"

"Why Monica or why you?" Richard asked.

She put a hand on the table to steady herself. "Both."

"Because it just fell in my lap. I've got a money-grubbing wife I can't divorce because of a prenup. Then my former mistress—sorry, *girlfriend*—shows up. On our island. Without my hand in it at all. It was the perfect setup. The whole scenario just needed a little shove from me—" He mimed one finger knocking over a domino. "—and I was in business. I get out of this torture of a marriage without losing a cent and you take the blame. I couldn't have planned it better myself."

A black, guttural laugh burst from him. "She thought she was planning my birthday but actually," he laughed harder, "she *planned* her own murder."

Addie's mouth dropped, stunned by his brutal heartlessness. "It won't work," she managed to whisper. "They won't believe you."

He shrugged. "They will. Trust me. I've planted enough evidence to make your"—he made air quotes—"'plan,' clear to everyone. Breaking up with me like that in that restaurant was a mistake. You should have *never* embarrassed me in public. I don't tolerate disrespect. *Ever*." He spat the last word. "That was mistake number one. Mistake number two was taking Monica up on her ridiculous offer."

"Richard, please—"

"I think it's time I call the police. After all, you've just murdered someone."

At those words, everything froze. Addie. Richard. Time. Suddenly, through the incapacitating fog of disbelief, one shining thought emerged.

Run.

20

ADDIE

Addie burst through the kitchen door. It swung back violently as she scanned the room for her phone to no avail.

It was right here on the counter, right next to my notes! I saw it!

When, though? She hadn't looked at it for close to an hour. She had been in the zone, cooking, focusing on her iPad notes... She *had* gone to the bathroom. Had she taken it with her and left it—

Richard's palm smacked the door, stopping it from swinging before he pushed through. "Addie, there's no point—"

Before he finished, Addie reached for the knife block, her fingers fumbling across several handles before firmly grasping one and yanking it out. She held it up between them, warning him off.

"Addie, come on. You're not going to use that."

The island was between them, enough of a barrier—she guessed—to allow her to reach the doorway to the living room before he would reach her. But she needed to go in the other direction, past the island to the short hall off the kitchen that held the laundry room and bathroom she had used. The problem was, not only was that on Richard's side of the island, the hall was a dead end. If her phone wasn't in the bathroom, she would have no way to call for help and would be stuck with nowhere to go.

Then she spotted her iPad on the island. She lunged for it, but he was too fast, yanking it away before she reached it. She reversed her trajectory before he grabbed her too.

"Ah-ah-ah," he taunted, wagging a finger at her. "Now hand over your phone."

Her insides did a loop. Something in her eyes must have given her away because he grinned. "Oh," he said, his shoulders dropping as a knowing look joined the grin, "you don't have your phone."

She couldn't get past him and he had her iPad. Which left only one option.

She made for the doorway to the living room, darting straight through it, headed for the main stairs, praying Richard wouldn't be fast enough to grab her. She expected to feel a leg or ankle wrenched back by his grasp, or her hair yanked, but she ran unhindered all the way. Her heart banged against her ribs as she flew up the steps, tripping a couple of times when her shoes caught on the bullnose edges. Each time she fell she gasped, starting up again with a grunt, furious she couldn't rein herself in enough to run properly when her life depended on it.

She was halfway up the first flight, when she realized she didn't hear him. No heavy steps pounding after her. No angry shouts calling her name. Nothing.

Where is he?!

Not knowing the answer to that question was terrifying.

Without stopping, she chanced a quick look over her shoulder. She tripped again but managed to confirm he wasn't behind her before regaining her footing and continuing upward.

The Offer

Why isn't he coming after me? What is he planning?!

Not knowing the answer to those questions was more terrifying than not knowing where he was. He had clearly thought this all through. If he wasn't following her, there would be a reason. One that wouldn't be good for her.

I have to make it to my room.

She charged higher, despite her instincts screaming that staying inside the house was insane and that she should run out the front door and keep going until she was as far from Richard as possible. The problem was, those instincts didn't take into consideration that she was on an island. One that was only so big. In the end, where could she go where she wouldn't be found eventually? She might be able to hide, but for how long? Plus, she had no phone. No way to reach the outside world. Logic fought against instinct, insisting her only chance lay in using her laptop, which was in her bedroom, to call for help.

Out of breath and panting, Addie hit the third-floor landing and sprinted to her room. She shoved the door open, hurtled inside, and locked it behind her. Relief swept through her when she spotted her laptop still on the bed where she had left it. She snatched it up and flung open the screen, her brief relief replaced by another swell of panic when she saw that the three little radio signal lines indicating the laptop's Wi-Fi status had a line marked through them.

Her computer wasn't connected to Wi-Fi any longer. Which meant she couldn't use it to reach out for help.

Typing frantically, she selected the network again and entered the password Monica had given her, but not before having to backspace and retype it several times before entering it correctly. After a few seconds, a message appeared.

The network SpiritsIsland-1 requires a WPA2 password.

"That *is* the password!" Addie yelled at the laptop, trying the password again. Her stomach dropped several stories when it didn't work. She started to type it again when the sound of slow, heavy steps from somewhere in the hallway met her ears, bringing her fingers to a halt. She looked at the door, a savage bout of queasiness rocking her as the steps thumped closer and closer.

"This actually works out pretty well," Richard called out as the door handle jiggled then fell still. Addie thought of the simple button lock on the handle and knew it wouldn't keep him out, not if he really wanted to get in. If he got in...she had the knife, but he was right. She wasn't prepared to stab anyone. Not even Richard. Not unless it was her only way to stay alive.

Think, Addie. Think.

The handle wasn't moving anymore, and though she heard more steps, they sounded as if they were headed away from the room, farther down the hallway.

What is he doing?

The answer came in loud grinding noises, like wood against wood. Bumps and bangs ensued. He was moving something.

Addie tried to focus, but she was looking at everything through a panicked haze. She couldn't think clearly. She needed to come up with a plan, but instead, she was just sitting there, too paralyzed to act.

What is wrong with you? You have to do something!

Her pulse pounded in her ears and heat flushed her face. She pressed her hands against her cheeks and shook her head. She was running out of time.

Think!

Suddenly something clicked. A cog fell into place.

My pepper spray.

Addie dove for her purse and plunged her hand inside. Her

frantic whine pierced the air as her fingers came out of the bag's depth, empty.

Her pepper spray was gone too. He had thought of everything.

She scanned the room for something—anything—less lethal than a knife that she could use to fight him off once he finally made it inside. Because he *would* make it inside. All it took to open the simple lock was a bent paperclip, and she was certain Richard was prepared for that. But there wasn't anything easy to wield that would do enough damage to hold him back.

It was the knife or nothing.

Lightning flashed, followed by a boom of thunder. Addie's gaze shifted to the window. She was too high up for it to be a safe escape option even in the best weather. In this storm, the rain would make scaling the wall and the roof of the porch treacherous if not impossible. Still, she would have a better chance running than trying to defend herself against Richard with a knife. He was so much stronger than she was. He was just as likely to take the knife away and turn it on her.

If only she could make it outside and hide long enough, Sam might be able to help her when he returned tomorrow for Tanya—

Tanya!

Her palm smacked her forehead. Why hadn't she thought of her already? Tanya was still in the guest cottage, where Monica had sent her until Sam picked her up tomorrow afternoon! Tanya would have a phone!

But Richard knew about Tanya.

Had Richard done something with Tanya? Would he have left her alone out in the cottage? How could he know she wouldn't come back to the main house and spoil everything? If Richard was willing to kill Monica, would he have left that loose end dangling?

Overwhelming concern for Tanya sent electric jolts over her skin.

Wait, though. Something happening to Tanya would completely undermine the story Richard intends to present to the police—that I'm the killer, out to get Monica, and planned to make Monica's death look like a suicide. In that scenario, I wouldn't have a reason to kill Tanya. Just the opposite, because Tanya's death would be one too many, putting a big question mark over Monica's supposed suicide.

So Tanya was probably safe. In fact, Richard probably planned to call her back now that the deed was done. He was probably hoping to use her as an additional witness.

Probably.

Probably wasn't good enough. What if this theory was wrong? What if Tanya was in danger?

Addie couldn't just assume Tanya would be all right. She would have to try to reach her before Richard did. Not only to warn her but to check the cottage for a landline. During their house tour, Monica had mentioned the house didn't have one.

More bumping and creaking sounded from the hallway. Addie forced herself to focus as another wave of lightheadedness struck.

You need to push something against the door.

The vanity was the only piece of substantial furniture not too heavy to move. She started to drag it over, intending to brace it under the handle to keep the door from opening, when Richard called out, "Okay, Addie, get comfortable. I've got some things to take care of before I call the police, and then it'll take them a while to get here."

Addie froze, realization crystallizing.

He isn't trying to break in.

He's trapping me inside.

She stepped back, slightly unsteady on her feet. She took a deep breath trying to calm herself. "This isn't going to work, Richard!" she yelled.

He laughed. "Yes, it will."

The Offer

"No, it won't. Think about it. Take the story you're planning on telling the police, that I killed Monica to free us to be together. What would I have done if you refused to take me back? Huh? If that were my plan, I'd be stuck! You'd be alive to tell them what I did and it would all be over. That plan doesn't make sense."

He snorted. "It does if your Plan B was to overdose me on the same meds if I didn't cooperate. Right now, a bottle of my favorite scotch is in my study downstairs. I've laced it with the same meds I used on Monica. Of course, to the police it'll appear you were the one who doctored the scotch. It'll look like your plan was to let me drink it if I didn't go along with you. You know how much I love my scotch and figured I'd be so shaken I'd be reaching for a drink as soon as possible. It wouldn't be hard to anticipate. And it won't be hard for them to believe."

"No one is going to believe that was my plan! That plan gives me no way out. At the very least I'd have no explanation for your death and I'd end up in prison, for at least one murder, if not two."

"You're wrong. That plan makes complete sense if your story was going to be that Monica pre-poisoned my scotch before committing suicide. That way I'd die after her, leaving you to take all the blame and go to prison in a final act of revenge against her philandering husband and his mistress."

"That's idiotic!"

"Not every criminal is a genius. You were just a stupid woman, blinded by jealousy, desperate to either have me or kill me. That's what I'll say, anyway. I'll have to take a sip of the scotch—just a little one, that's barely dosed—before conveniently realizing it isn't a good idea to drink anything in the house after what you did to Monica. When the drug shows up in my system and in the bottle, that should seal the deal."

The handle jiggled again and creaking sounded from the other side of the door.

"Don't get any ideas about going out the window. It's a three-story drop. And forget the door. I used to use this trick on Keeley and Justin all the time as teenagers when they got unmanageable. You're not getting out of here." He clicked his tongue, his superiority complex seeping through from the other side of the door. "Who would have guessed? Addie Nichols, a murderer. I guess you never know about people."

"Richard!"

But he was done talking to her. His footfalls thumped again, this time moving away from the door in the direction of the stairs. When they faded, she unlocked the door and yanked hard on the handle. Though it turned, she couldn't pull the door open even an inch. All she managed was a gap barely wide enough to see through when she pressed her eye to it. What looked like a terry-cloth robe tie was tightly looped around the door handle on one end, then pulled taut over the top of a large mahogany chest braced against the door—the item Richard must have been moving in the hall. She guessed the other end of the tie was secured to some part of the chest, holding the door tight against it, preventing it from being opened inward.

Inside the room, Addie sunk down on the floor against the door, her head in her hands. She tried to focus on calming down, closing her eyes, slowing her breathing, and imagining her diaphragm moving out and in. She filled her lungs through her nose with new air untainted by fear, then blew out the anxiety-ridden air through her mouth.

God, please help me. He's got me backed in a corner, and if he's right—if he's framed me well enough—they're going to believe him. I'm in so much trouble. Please help me.

She took another few deep breaths and opened her eyes. Her gaze fell on the laptop again.

The evidence.

The Offer

She scrambled to the bed and opened her email account, scanning it for anything she didn't recognize. It didn't take long to find something. More perspiration broke out on her forehead as she found numerous "sent" messages dated over the last several weeks that she had never seen. Messages she had never written. All saved alongside her genuine "sent" emails, as if they had been sent from her account.

Richard, I miss you so much. I'm so sorry I got so angry. Please take me back...

Richard, I know you didn't mean it. You couldn't have meant it. Please take me back...

Richard, I won't let you leave me like this. You're supposed to leave her. I don't believe any of this about you making your marriage work. If you don't reconsider, you'll be sorry. She'll be sorry...

There were also emails from him telling her it was over between them. To leave him alone. To stop begging him to take her back. Insisting their relationship had been a mistake and he wanted to repair his marriage.

He hadn't been lying. Someone had hacked her email and planted these messages, which must have auto-downloaded before the Wi-Fi password was changed.

She could delete them. But as soon as the police pulled up her account on the server, they would see these incriminating messages. So if she did delete them on her laptop, it would look like she was trying to hide something.

Better to leave them and argue that they supported the truth, that she had been hacked. She tossed the laptop aside and tried to focus on what Richard had said about framing her. Specifically, the part about the emails not being the only incriminating proof.

The medication residue.

Addie grabbed her purse and dumped it onto the bed. With a faint tremor in her hands, she briskly scanned the contents, flipping through them, opening the zipper in her wallet and the lids on her makeup.

Nothing.

She grabbed her duffel and dumped it out too. Rummaging through that pile of belongings also turned up nothing. Addie yanked the opening of the duffel wide, holding it up so as much light as possible illuminated the interior.

White grit, the consistency of powdered candy, ran along one of the bottom seams. Addie's hands started to shake. There was no way to get the residue out altogether. Plus, washing it in the bathroom sink would leave traces behind that the police could likely still detect. Not to mention that, just like erasing emails, washing the duffel out would only make her look more guilty. Like she was trying to hide something.

What was he going to claim? That she had stolen Monica's medication and crushed it up? That she had hidden it in her duffel bag—where some had spilled out without her realizing it—and used the crushed medication to overdose them?

Yes. That's exactly what he would say had happened. Unless she found something to prove he was behind it all, they would believe him.

Now, thinking back on the events of the evening, so many things made sense. Like why Richard made sure he was the one who made Monica's last drink.

No wonder he was so helpful. It's how he slipped the meds in.

Monica always had at least a gimlet or two before dinner. She had told Addie that and Monica's behavior the night before had

The Offer

borne that out. The drugs would be guaranteed to get in her system that way. Despondency gripped Addie. *She* had made Monica's first gimlet.

My fingerprints are all over her glass. But so are his, aren't they?

She vaguely recalled him grabbing napkins when he had carried the first drink to Monica. Had he brought it back like that too, made her another gimlet, then carried it to her, still holding it with a napkin? She couldn't remember. Given how well he planned this out, she guessed he had. If that was the case, Addie's and Monica's fingerprints would be the only ones on her glass.

Richard had thought of everything. The police would be there soon and they would believe what he told them. Because why wouldn't they, when the evidence all matched up with what Richard was going to say? When he was going so far as to drug himself with the laced scotch—just a little bit—to convincingly sell his version of the story?

She needed to get out of that room. She needed a phone and a chance to search the place, to find some evidence proving what Richard had done. She could search his office. His bedroom. Find something incriminating before he got rid of it all. He was so confident right now. That might work to her advantage. She might even overhear something useful. If he happened to confess...

Confess!

Addie wanted to smack herself. Richard *had* just confessed.

I sat there, yelling at him instead of recording it.

Her laptop had been in the room the whole time and for some reason it hadn't occurred to her to record him. She wasn't stupid, so it had to have been the shock. Maybe it wasn't too late. If she moved quickly, there was a chance she could use her laptop to record him now. Maybe she could catch him doing something, anything, that wouldn't match up with the tale he planned to tell. Or, if nothing else, as a last resort maybe she could hide the laptop within earshot, then provoke him into making another admission.

Even as she considered these possibilities, she knew the chances of success at any of them were less than slim. She was grasping at straws. But what else could she do? She had nothing else to cling to. She had to try *something*. And she had to get to Tanya and Tanya's phone.

If the door was barred, the window, however dangerous, was her only way out. Sheets of heavy rain cascaded past the glass, so much so that the river she had admired that morning was no longer visible. She could only imagine how slippery it would be outside, but she would have to try.

I can knot the sheets, tie them into ropes, and Rapunzel it down.

It wasn't much of a plan, but it was all she had. She snagged one of the bedsheets as the booming crack of a gunshot split the air.

21

ADDIE

Addie's body seized, a new level of fear gripping her.
He's got a gun.
Her heart pounded...boom...boom...boom.
He's not holding me for the police. He's going to kill me and claim he shot me in self-defense.

Addie darted back to the door, now even more wobbly on her feet. She locked it again and jammed the vanity up under the handle. She leaned against it, her chest heaving with sharp, quick breaths, until it occurred to her that in that position she was a sitting duck, directly in the path of any shots Richard might fire through the door. She stepped to the side.

Lord, please protect me.

Addie brushed a renegade tear from her cheek, hating that it was there. She had to be strong. She had to be smart. Fight back. Escape. But he had all the advantages of pre-planning. Plus, her own body was failing her, crumbling under the shock, both physically and mentally. She couldn't make another mistake like failing to record him. She needed to figure out what he was doing, or she wasn't going to make it.

If he plans to kill me, why is he firing a gun in another part of the house? All it does is warn me something's coming.

So why did he shoot?

Her mind was a swirling mess. She closed her eyes, a desperate longing to be gone filling every space of her. A crying need to be away from here. To be unaware. If only this was a nightmare. If only she could wake from it, roll over, and go back to sleep.

Sleep.

"No!" she barked at herself, shuddering as her lids flew open and she blinked purposefully.

The drowsiness her system was trying to use as a defense mechanism wasn't a defense at all. It would be the death of her. She had to focus.

Richard had been five steps ahead of her this whole time. There would be a reason he shot that gun. She needed to move. Now.

Addie began working on the top sheet, hurriedly tying knots along its length. When she finished, she ripped off the fitted sheet and did the same. She tied them together, disappointed to find the makeshift rope was less than ten feet long. She might be able to lower herself as far as the next floor down, but what after that? Drop a whole story? If she broke an ankle or a leg, she wouldn't have a chance. Then again, she wouldn't have a chance if she stayed. She needed to get out and try to secure proof of what Richard had done, then hide until the police arrived.

It was now or never. Addie listened for Richard's heavy steps, hoping to get a sense of how close he might be and how much time she had.

There was nothing. No more gunfire, no steps, and no taunting words from a confident Richard. No indication of life outside her door at all.

Instinct fired within her. Something wasn't right about this.

The gun...maybe it wasn't about her. A nauseating heat rippled under her skin as her hand flew to her mouth.

Oh, no. No, no, no.

Tanya.

Had she come back to the house early? Had she stumbled into a crime scene only to become part of it? If Tanya surprised Richard in the act of setting the stage or foiled his plan somehow, would he have shot her even though it would put his story in doubt?

Maybe, if he didn't have a choice.

If he had, he would devise a way to blame that on Addie too.

None of this was Tanya's fault. It wasn't Addie's either, but if another innocent woman was down there right now, bleeding to death, she couldn't leave her. She had to do something to help her.

Even if it meant Addie didn't get away.

She would get him up there. Trick him somehow into the room and use the knife. If she survived, she could help Tanya, if that was what the gunshot was about, and if Tanya wasn't in danger, she would run. If she didn't survive, at least she would die trying to help someone.

Addie heaved the vanity out of the way. "Richard!" she screamed, banging her fist on the door. "Richard, what's going on?" When he didn't answer, she seized the handle with both hands to rattle the door as hard as she could.

At the first twist and yank, the door gave with a burst of force, unexpectedly swinging inward. Addie flew back, tripping over her feet and landing hard on the floor. For several seconds she stared in disbelief at the open door before scrambling up, grabbing the knife and laptop off the bed, and racing to the doorway.

22

ADDIE

Addie didn't stop to wonder why or how the restraint on the door had suddenly come loose, or whether that was a good or bad thing. Tanya's welfare was the only thing that mattered at the moment. She leaned against the chest Richard had shoved against the door and swung her head left and right. The hallway was empty. If someone had loosened the tie, they were gone now.

Addie hoisted herself up and over the chest then ran to the landing at the end of the hall. She peered over the railing. No one was on the flight below. She crept down, keeping her steps soft—though she wasn't sure it would make any difference given the racket she had made before realizing she could get out. She held the knife at the ready, listening and watching for any sign of movement. At the second-story landing, she looked over the railing to check the next flight down.

Empty again.

Addie slinked down to the first floor and stepped off the last stair into the living room. Richard had said he would be in his study, tasting the scotch, then calling the police. She pictured him in there now. It was easy. The night before she had seen him through the glass French doors leading directly into the study from the back of the living room, sitting behind his desk, pouring from the bottle. But she couldn't enter that way. She needed to get a look at what was going on without him seeing her. She needed the element of surprise. So instead she turned down the hallway leading down the side of the study, to the rooms in the right wing of the house.

The stream of adrenaline coursing through her had catapulted her nervous system into hyperdrive. The floor wobbled, and she blinked rapidly, willing it to stop.

Concentrate. Stay in control.

She had to find Richard. She had to know what the gunshot was about. She clutched the laptop to her chest. If possible, she would try to record him doing something incriminating, though how she would surreptitiously do that with a laptop she couldn't imagine. Recording him was secondary to making certain Tanya was all right —that either she wasn't in the house, or, if she was, that she wasn't in danger.

Addie passed a bathroom on the left without encountering a soul. The first door on the right was to Richard's study and it was open. She pressed herself against the wall, took a deep breath, and leaned in just enough to peek inside. Her hand flew to her mouth, stifling a scream as a shiver tore through her frame.

Richard lay sprawled on the floor, his hand uselessly clutching his chest, a great red stain flowering beneath his fingers.

Addie's mind whirled, reality swayed, and she had to steady herself by bracing against a chair to keep from toppling.

Someone had shot Richard, not the other way around.

And she had no idea where they were.

Addie scanned the room, an acute awareness of her vulnerability striking her like a bolt of lightning. She dropped down, making a smaller target of herself, scooting toward Richard.

"Richard?" she hissed, keeping low, now close to his head. "What happened? Who did this?"

His eyes were fixated on something beyond her, but shifted at the sound of her voice, finding hers. "Ad...die...can't..." A labored breath spilled from his lips, his eyelids closing and opening, but not seeming to focus.

"Who shot you? Where are they?" Her whispers were harsh and urgent, but she needed answers. "Are they still here?" When he didn't respond, she put down both the knife and the laptop, grabbed his shoulder and shook it. "Richard, please!"

His gaze drifted, falling on a second set of double doors behind them that led to an outdoor patio. Was that intentional? Was he trying to tell her something?

"Are they out there?" Addie asked, angling herself so she was facing the direction he was looking. "Who is it?"

"It...I..." Before he got the rest of the sentence out, his head lolled to one side and his hand stopped quivering. Addie patted his cheek.

"Richard? Richard?"

It was no use. His stare had left this earth.

Addie rose, stumbling back to lean against the chair again. Her eyes darted left and right as another, stronger wave of lightheadedness hit, threatening to overtake her. Her galloping lungs pushed her to the verge of hyperventilation.

Calm down, Addie. You have to think. You can't pass out.

Think.

Hope burst in her chest as an answer came. She slipped back to Richard. Shutting out the fact that she was searching a dead man, and how her stomach contracted dangerously at that reality, Addie

The Offer

fumbled through his pockets. He would have a phone. He would have *her* phone. She could make a call. She could get help.

But there was no phone. Not his. Not hers. Her head snapped to his desk. No phones on the desktop or anywhere within view.

Hope evaporated.

Two people were dead. Now it would look like she had killed them both. The authorities would believe *she* was a murderer. She sat back on her heels, trying to make sense of this impossible situation.

Richard was the villain here. He killed Monica. He planned to frame me. So, then who killed—

Understanding burned through her consciousness, like a headlight through fog, and she shot up, her skin tingling.

Richard had been killed by the only other person on this island.

And Addie was stuck on it with her.

Alone.

23

NOT ADDIE

Everything was working out.
This is it. The big finale. The curtain call.
It hasn't all gone according to plan. I mean, talk about a twist.
But in the end, it had only helped the situation. Only framed Adelaide Nichols more tidily.
Poor Addie.
Wrong place, wrong time. Wrong man.
Wrong wife.
She should have known better than to take the money. If it's too good to be true...
She heard her, begging Richard for answers, her voice trembling. The woman was a rabbit caught in its burrow, knowing full well the fox prowled right outside. Waiting to pounce.
If she was afraid now, she was about to be absolutely terrified.

24

ADDIE

The only other person on this island, the only other person left alive, was Tanya. Now instead of being terrified *for* her, Addie was terrified *of* her.

Addie's gaze rolled over Richard's desk, to where his laptop sat open. She ran to it, her heart plummeting when she saw it displayed the home screen, which was password protected. Ripping open the desk drawer, she searched for anything that might prove his guilt or her innocence, or get her off the island.

Passwords. Another phone. Keys to the boat.

The boat that doesn't work.

Addie slammed the drawer shut. This was pointless. She wasn't getting off this island. Hiding was her only option and she needed to do it fast. Tanya had a gun and—

Addie's gut fluttered as another realization struck her, this one encouraging.

The gun that killed Richard doesn't have my fingerprints on it.

It wasn't much, but it was something. Something that would hopefully make it clear to the authorities that there was more to the situation than met the eye. Enough to encourage the police to ask questions. To maybe even believe her.

Although, getting my fingerprints on the gun is probably something she plans to make happen.

Tanya would need that evidence if she was going to succeed in framing Addie. Addie wasn't willingly going to put her hand on that gun. Which meant Tanya either had to incapacitate her or kill her to tie this up neatly. The easiest thing would be for Tanya to make it look like a double murder and suicide. Make Addie the woman scorned, so jealous that she killed her boyfriend, his wife, and herself. It could work.

But only if Addie was dead.

Is Tanya capable of killing me, an innocent person in whatever is happening here? For that matter, what motive can she possibly have for any of it?

The answer came as if it had been tucked away in her mind, waiting to be called upon. Richard had made it clear Addie wasn't the only woman he had dated while married. Maybe Tanya was one of his other girlfriends, scorned and out for revenge. It would explain why Tanya had shown up when Monica was certain she had canceled her services for that weekend. If Tanya thought no one else would be here besides Monica and Richard, she might have decided it would be the perfect time to get even.

Why are you standing here, playing twenty questions?

It doesn't matter what the reason is. The woman has a gun. You need to move.

A hushed groan crawled out of Addie's throat. She didn't know what to do. Should she stay in the house or head outside? If she ventured outside, what then? She didn't know the island at all. She would be running blind. Addie grabbed her forehead where a monster headache was slicing through her brain, making it harder to think.

Focus on what you know, Addie. Focus on what you know.

One thing she was sure of was that she wasn't safe inside. Tanya could be anywhere and she didn't want to end up trapped in the same room with her.

The patio doors weren't an option after the way Richard had looked at them, possibly trying to tell her Tanya was out there. Addie grabbed the knife and her laptop, then bolted through the same door she had entered the study through. Once in the hallway, she raced toward the front door, the closest exit from the house. She had just rocketed past the stairs when a haunting sound brought her legs—and nearly her heart—to a full stop.

25

ADDIE

"Aaa-deee-laaide?"

A voice. A woman's voice, calling out in a sing-song lilt sending shivers down Addie's spine.

Tanya.

Addie spun on the spot, unable to tell where the voice was coming from, other than from somewhere further in the house. Beyond that, she couldn't pinpoint it.

Had the voice come from the foyer, closer to the front door than she was now? Or from one of the rooms along the hall? Or maybe Tanya had backtracked to the study.

Addie swallowed hard, pressing back the dizziness threatening to overtake her.

Maybe she's coming up behind me right now.

Swells of sweaty panic broke over Addie as she ran to the only place she was certain Tanya's voice *hadn't* come from.

The Offer

This is a mistake. This is a mistake.

The thought echoed in Addie's head as she took one flight, then another, trying to run and think through an escape at the same time. She considered jumping out a second-story window, but Tanya's voice ringing behind her propelled her upward.

"Addie, there's no point in running," Tanya taunted from somewhere below. "There's nowhere to go. Inside, outside. Upstairs or down, I'll find you. You're only making this harder."

Addie pushed herself to pick up the pace. Her breathing was labored, her energy drained as she processed on the run. Halfway up the second flight, her foot missed a stair and she tripped. Both the laptop and knife tumbled out of her hands as she grabbed for the rail to catch herself. They slid back down the stairs and out of reach. She couldn't go back for them. Tanya was too close. With a frustrated whimper, Addie resumed climbing, her mind still running through her options.

She couldn't hide in her room. It would be one of the first places Tanya checked. Really, any of the rooms would be a dead end. It wouldn't take Tanya long to search them all. The daunting reality of her situation stole over her, weakness creeping farther into her limbs. Tanya was right. No matter where she hid, she would ultimately be found out.

Think, think, think! God please, give me an answer. An idea. Anything.

"Aaa-deee-laaide...come on. I promise it won't hurt."

Tanya wasn't far behind her. She was closer than Addie had realized downstairs. Which meant, if Addie *had* attempted to leave by way of the front door, she wouldn't have made it. Going upstairs had been the right decision.

Now she just needed to make another one. And that was when it hit her.

The story Sam told her about the hidden cabinet.

Would Tanya know about it?

Even if she did, she wouldn't think Addie knew about it. It might be one of the last places Tanya would look. Unless Addie wanted to crawl out a window and take her chances with a jump, the cabinet might be her best bet. It was also on the highest floor, hopefully, the last one Tanya would search. Addie needed it to be the last one. Every second meant a little more time for help to arrive, though she couldn't think of how that would happen without a phone.

Time and concealment were her best defenses right now. Moving as quickly as she could without making noise, she crossed the next landing and continued up toward the fifth floor.

26

NOT ADDIE

"Aaa-deee-laaide?" She projected the haunting, sing-song taunt, knowing it would reach Addie wherever she had scurried off to. Based on the footsteps that betrayed someone running in a panic, she was guessing the third or fourth floor. They were the most likely choices given all the small rooms on those levels—half a dozen bedrooms, the accompanying baths, and all those closets. Plenty of places for someone to hide.

But not for long.

"Aaa-deee-laaide? Are you ignoring me?"

The heavy footfalls had stopped, leaving only silence in the house and the thundering storm outside. Would Addie be able to tell where she was based on the sound of her voice?

Probably not.

She imagined the woman balled up, hugging her knees, hiding in the dark in the back of some closet. She would check those first.

Thunder boomed and the heavens opened wider, sending another roaring deluge of angry rain onto the mansion. She grinned. The storm had been helpful. It had limited Addie's options to trying to survive inside the house. Outside Addie would have been stumbling around in torrents of rain in the darkness and leaving tracks in the wet earth. Which left the house as the only viable hiding place.

Much easier for me.

She searched the first bedroom she came to, ripping open the closet doors. Nothing but spare robes for guests.

How thoughtful. Not that I ever got to use one.

She checked under the bed, the shower, and the linen closet in the private bath. Again, no Addie. She headed to the next bedroom and repeated the process.

"Are you pretending you can't hear me?" she bellowed when she came up empty after the third room, frustration burgeoning. Addie had gotten a lead on her when she had to run down to the dock to check on lights approaching from the river, afraid it might be the boat taxi returning for some reason. Fortunately, it turned out to be a random boater, apparently caught out in the storm, hugging the shore to get back to wherever they were going, but the delay had resulted in this high-stakes game of hide-and-seek. It shouldn't be much of a problem, as long as it ended soon. She had a timeline to keep if all the evidence was going to line up and point the way she needed it to once the police started asking questions.

She took a deep breath, focused on hearing her heartbeat and slowing it. Addie was trapped. She couldn't reach an exit without running right past her.

"You can't hiiiii-de from me. Not forrr-ehh-ver, Adelaide!" She hoped the taunting was unnerving Addie bit by bit and might push her to make the stupid decision to run. "I'll find you eventually! I will!"

The Offer

Please try it now. Make a run for it. It'll make it so much easier for me.

"You should have taken your chances outside. At least you'd have given yourself a shot."

She cocked her head, working to listen past the pounding rain to detect the slightest disturbance inside the house. Though it had likely kept Addie inside, one disadvantage of the rain was it drowned out the sound of any movement she might be making.

"The storm would have at least made you harder to find!" she called out. "This house might be big, but there are only so many rooms to hide in!" She paused, letting that sink into Addie's brain, then started again.

"Come ooouu-t, come ooouu-t, wherever you are. Aaa-deee-laaide..."

27

ADDIE

Addie was hyperventilating. Or at least it felt that way. Each breath she sucked in seemed to come quicker and be less filling than the last. She closed her eyes.
Breathe in. 1-2-3-4. Breathe out. 1-2-3-4.
It helped a little.
A little.
She prayed again. Still, Tanya's voice kept coming.
Addie pressed harder into the back of the cabinet as if she could somehow retreat further into it. She still couldn't believe she managed to find the little lever under the trim that popped open the door to the hidden cabinet. It was in the center of the two-foot-high base of the built-in bookshelves stretching from floor to ceiling. Though the base appeared to be a solid foundation, in reality, the middle of the three separate sections held the hiding place Sam had spoken of.

The Offer

Addie had barely managed to fit inside the low, cramped compartment. Using an interior strap, she had pulled the door shut behind her and tried to arrange her limbs in a position that didn't ache excruciatingly. She had failed. Every joint throbbed after the long day on her feet, and being twisted like a pretzel only made it worse. Her head was bent at an odd angle, sending a persistent pulsating pain down the side of her neck. She shifted, hoping to placate the nerve, when something stung her in the back. Thoughts of black widow spiders sent her heart galloping and, unable to stop herself, she reached back and grabbed the spot.

It wasn't a spider.

A splinter was coming loose from the back of the cabinet. She pulled hard on it, intending to rip it off so she wouldn't impale herself on it again. A larger piece than expected, an actual strip of wood, tore away, followed by a feeble waft of air caressing her face.

What?

She ran her hands over the strip, estimating it to be an inch wide. Traveling along the edge of the gap left by the strip, her fingers discovered that the back of the cabinet was, in actuality, nothing but a thin panel, not heavy oak like the rest of the bookcase, maybe a quarter-inch thick at most.

No...this...this couldn't be a way out, could it?

Addie urgently palpated the edges of the panel, seeking a way to remove it, perhaps with a lever similar to the one that opened the compartment door. Her heart leapt when her fingers detected another small piece of wood where the top edge of the panel met the top of the compartment. It felt a lot like the hidden lever on the outside of the bookcase. She wiggled it and it moved, rotating outward ninety degrees, but nothing else happened. Inside her head, a ticking clock counted down, driving her pulse higher. Expecting to hear footsteps at any moment, she shoved against the back panel, praying something—anything—would happen.

A crack sounded and the panel gave, falling away into whatever lay beyond in the darkness.

28

NOT ADDIE

I nearly forgot about this room.
Its existence was an easy thing to forget, as the stairs were at the far end of the hall concealed behind a door that looked like a closet, and she rarely entered it. At first, when Addie hadn't been in any of the fourth-floor rooms, she had been gripped by a few tense moments of worry that Addie had somehow slipped past her to the floors below. Then she remembered the room at the top.

After climbing the short flight of stairs, she stepped into the room, with its wide bay window and bookcases stretching to the ceiling, ears pricked for any misplaced sound. This close to the roof, though, the downpour was like a herd of elephants charging across the shingles.

It didn't matter. The circular room held only two leather armchairs, a rug, a side table, and a lamp. There was nowhere to hide.

Nowhere except for the hidden compartment in the base of the old bookcase.

29

ADDIE

This wasn't just a hiding place.

It was an escape passage.

A few seconds passed between the panel falling away and it clattering on the bottom of wherever this exposed space led, so the drop had to be fairly deep. There was no way to know precisely how deep, or into what it descended, because, as in the compartment, there was no light—only darkness and the smell of mildew, age, and decaying things. The one bright spot was that the slight breeze tickling her cheek suggested it must lead somewhere.

Which meant she had a chance.

Addie reached into the open space and groped around. As best she could tell, it was a chute of sorts. There was a surface directly opposite her, a little farther away than arm's length. Two other surfaces came off that one at ninety-degree angles, boxing out the chute and creating a space somewhat wider than the compartment.

Each surface—walls for the lack of a better term—seemed to be lined with rough wooden panels, very old and very weathered by the feel of them and the splinters piercing her skin. The wall directly across from her had rungs attached, like a built-in ladder. Stretching as far as she could, she felt two rungs descending from the top. There was no way to know if there were more rungs below that.

Or if it's safe.

Sam didn't mention this passage, but did that mean the previous owner didn't tell him about it, or that he didn't know about it either? If the last owner hadn't known about it, maybe no one had for some time. In that case, the rungs might not have borne weight for a century or more. Would they hold her or send her crashing to the bottom?

A creak sounded from the direction of the room.

Tanya was coming. She would have to take her chances.

Addie reached for the first rung and pulled on it hard, her spirit lifting when it held. Grabbing on with both hands, she worked herself through the narrow opening, one leg dangling for a moment before her foot found a lower rung. She expelled a relieved sigh.

Now if they'll just hold me.

Pressing herself against the wall and praying the rungs wouldn't snap off, she started her trek into the dark. Afraid any aggressive shift might rip the ancient rungs right out of the wall, Addie carefully worked her way down, moving one hand at a time, one foot at a time. She descended what had to be at least three stories, if not more, when suddenly the rung under her left foot, the one bearing all her weight at that moment, broke away. Her fingers clawed at their rungs as she flailed about, her feet wildly scrambling for purchase. Before they found it, the rung in her right hand cracked and she plummeted into the void.

30

NOT ADDIE

She couldn't imagine that Addie knew about the compartment, but she had to rule it out. Someone might have told her about it or even shown it to her.

Moving to the center of the bookcase, she felt for the latch tucked beneath the decorative molding. She slid it over and the hidden door popped away from its frame. A shiver of anticipation flooded her as she stepped back, then kicked the door all the way open.

31

ADDIE

Addie hit the ground with a hard thump, pain shooting through her left foot. She yelped, grabbing it and rubbing her ankle vigorously.

Please not a break. Please.

Praying she had only twisted it at worst, she carefully shook her foot, then stood, gingerly putting weight on it. The ankle held her, though an angry ache complained.

Now at the bottom of...whatever this was, the scent of musty earth was overpowering. Darkness still enshrouded her. Addie closed her eyes and concentrated. A faint airflow brushed the left side of her face. She turned in that direction, crouching down to feel the ground beneath her.

Dirt.

Addie reached one hand out directly in front of her and found empty space as far as she was able to stretch. She raised her arm slowly. When it was level with her shoulder, the top of her knuckles hit a surface. She scooted closer and reached in, putting her palms against it. Her fingertips raked over what felt like brick with rough, uneven mortar in the joints. She followed the line of the brick. It formed an opening in the shape of an arch.

This was a tunnel.

A way out.

Shoving down thoughts of what might be crawling around in the passageway, she hunched over and stepped through, limping slightly, favoring her injured ankle as she went. To keep her bearings, she alternated between dragging her hands along the sides of the tunnel and waving them in front of her. Roots or vines—she couldn't tell which—snaked across the brick. Something wispy wrapped around one cheek and Addie clawed at what she knew had to be a spider web. Images of dime-sized arachnids hanging from her face erupted in her mind. Willing herself not to scream, she ran her hands over her face and shook them until she was as certain as she could be in the dark that nothing was on her. She swallowed the lump in her throat and kept moving, her heavy breathing the only sound.

Less than a minute later, the draft grew more pronounced and the faint sound of rain falling met her ears. Then her fingertips scraped a surface in front of her.

The end.

She reached out with both hands and discovered another wooden ladder. This one was shorter and propped against the wall at the end of the tunnel. She prayed it would hold, and started up, only to hit her head on something above her after scaling just two rungs.

The exit hatch.

Addie's pulse quickened as she pressed upward on the surface above her, hoping it was another lightweight wooden panel.

It wasn't. This was heavy. Probing the edges, she discovered a sliding bolt holding it in place. Addie unlocked it, bent her head down, braced her shoulders against the surface and shoved upward.

Nothing happened.

It wouldn't give. The thing was locked or stuck. Her mind ran wild with possibilities. Something might have been placed on top of it, or grown over it since it had likely sat unused for decades. Something might have fallen on it, or been built over it. She sucked in a quivering breath.

What if I can't get out?

Against rising panic and ignoring her burning ankle, she braced both hands and the top of her back on the hatch and shoved again.

This time it gave, rising a few inches. Addie stepped up one more rung, grunting as she heaved with all her might.

The hatch flung open on its hinges. Torrents of rain engulfed her as she crawled out of the tunnel, crying out in relief. She lay on the soaked earth, blinking in the scant, filtered moonlight which, after the pitch black of the tunnel, was like the sun. She rolled over to look back at where she had exited. The hatch was designed to lay flush with the ground when closed, though now it was open, propped against a small boulder. The top was completely caked in dirt and grass, likely accumulated over many years, and probably the reason it had been so hard to raise.

Trees and bushy undergrowth surrounded her. Addie pushed up off the ground and turned in a circle, working to get her bearings. The tunnel had dropped her out somewhere in the woods, but where exactly? Halfway around, she saw the topmost turret—the one that held the fifth-floor room—visible above the treetops, maybe thirty or forty yards away. So the passage had carried her somewhere behind the developed part of the property.

But was it far enough that she couldn't be seen from the turret room?

Addie closed the tunnel door, camouflaging it as best she could with dirt and grass, concealing it in case she needed to sneak back later to hide. The thought of holing up there was appealing and for a moment she considered going back inside right then to hide and wait. But wait for what? What help was coming? Plus, Tanya might know about the tunnel. It wasn't necessarily a secret to those regularly in the house.

Which meant her best bet was to run.

The rain pummeled her where she stood, her clothes hanging on her skin. A great shiver ripped through her as she pushed back a dripping swath of hair that had come loose from her ponytail. She tried to focus. To think. But she was so tired.

More than tired.

Exhausted. Spent. If she weren't so terrified, she might just crawl up next to the boulder beside the tunnel entrance and fall asleep, even in this storm. She couldn't, though. Stopping meant dying. She shook her head to stave off the exhaustion and worked to focus.

Think, Addie.

Tanya had been one step ahead of her this whole time. She had to assume that no matter where she went on the island, there was a good chance Tanya would find her and kill her. How long could she hope to stay hidden when Tanya knew the island better than she did? The earliest that help would arrive was late the next day when Sam came back to pick up the housekeeper. If Tanya caught up to her before then, and she likely would, Addie would end up dead. It wasn't hard to envision Tanya explaining the situation to the police, calling them to report the tragic murder-suicide scene she had "stumbled" onto in the main house.

Somehow, Tanya had discovered what Richard was doing and capitalized on it for reasons Addie didn't know. But if anyone could give someone a motive to murder them, it was Richard Farrow.

Something he had done had driven Tanya to kill him. And now Tanya was coming for her.

Staying would be suicide. Hiding, a dead end. She wouldn't be safe until she got off the island, and she could think of only one way to do it.

32

NOT ADDIE

Not only was the compartment empty, the back of it was gone. Black open space extended from where the rear surface should be. Shock rippled through her as she dropped to her knees, leaned into the compartment and shone the light from her phone into the hole.

It was some sort of chute, boxed out with very, *very,* old wood and what looked like similarly aged wooden rungs descending into whatever was below. She leaned in further, putting both the light and her head into the space.

The chute seemed to go all the way to the ground—down all five stories, if not lower. The light from the phone didn't go far enough for her to see what, or who, was at the bottom. She cocked her head, listening for anything indicating Addie was down there. All she heard was rain.

She slid out of the compartment, still on her knees, huffing as she swapped her phone for the gun in her pocket.

Now what?

Had Addie been in the compartment? Had she gone down that chute, or was it a coincidence that the back of it was gone? This contraption was a century or more old. The back side could have fallen out long ago.

Or Addie might have pushed it out.

Either way, Addie wasn't in this room.

She needed to get moving. Addie could be anywhere by now—maybe at the end of the chute wherever it led, or in the house, or even outside, headed for the water. It wouldn't have been hard for Addie to escape out the front door without being heard.

Will Addie decide to make a run for it outside? Or will she take her chances head-to-head, one-on-one, inside the house? Either way, it'll be much more of a challenge to find her now.

More of a challenge but not impossible. It was just the two of them on the island. No authorities. No help. She had hidden Addie's phone, along with the others, and because the Wi-Fi password had been changed, Addie wouldn't be able to reach anyone using a computer or tablet. It might take time, but finding Addie was *only* a matter of time.

She stood, resolution straightening her back and tensing her muscles. She would have to search the house again, this time in reverse from top to bottom. Urgency spurring her on, she stepped to the windows for a quick scan of the grounds before setting out to hunt inside the house, in case Addie had made it to the front lawn or had headed to the dock to try the boat.

A jolt of electricity fired down her spine when lightning revealed Addie, drenched to the bone, running across the grass toward the water.

33

ADDIE

Addie barreled around the side of the house, her foothold slipping in the mud as she turned the corner, almost sending her tumbling to the ground. She let out a whimper as her injured ankle wobbled. Despite the stab of pain, she righted herself and charged ahead, passing the turnoff to the dock, not sparing it—or the incapacitated boat—a look. Instead, her gaze focused on the only things that might save her now.

The kayaks.

The storm was bad, and the water rough, but Addie believed she had a better chance out on the river than staying on the island with a lunatic killer. Relief flooded her when she got close enough to spot paddles resting at the bottom of each of the kayaks.

This would work. She would make it to the next island. She had to.

She would use one kayak and push the other out so she couldn't be followed. Then, if Tanya noticed the crafts missing, she might think both kayaks floated away in the storm. Breathlessly, Addie came up fast on the first one and pushed it from its place along the shoreline, over the short stone retaining wall into the pounding waves, where it began floating away. Addie did the same with the other kayak, then jumped into the shoulder-high water, holding her breath against the relentless force of the swells as she climbed in the craft. Within seconds a whitecap hit her, violently rocking the kayak and almost capsizing her. Nerves firing, Addie grabbed the paddle and plunged it into the water.

I've got to move out of sight of the house.

If she remembered accurately from her trip over, the closest island was to the south, rather than back toward the marina. She dug the paddle in hard again and pulled, but terror gripped her when water rushed up over her back. She assumed a great swell had struck her, and turned in expectation of another.

The back end of the kayak was filling with water, sinking beneath the surface.

"No!" she screamed against the wind, forcefully changing the direction of her paddling to turn the kayak back to shore. When she reached the point where she could stand in the water, she jumped out and used every ounce of strength she had to drag the kayak back with her. She shoved it up onto the retaining wall, then, arms burning, pulled herself up beside it. She stood to get a better look at the bottom of the kayak and immediately knew what was wrong.

The bottom had been punctured with something—a hammer or knife—leaving slits Addie hadn't noticed in her rush to get away. Her gaze flicked up to the water, searching for the other kayak. It was gone, possibly carried away, but more likely, it had sunk. This was Tanya's doing. She destroyed the kayaks and then, instead of pushing them out to sink, left the crafts for anyone who came looking for them. The reason why made Addie tremble.

Tanya was attempting to do more than simply prevent an

escape.

She was using the kayaks as bait for anyone desperate to leave.

Panic surged. By going to the kayaks, Addie had put herself directly in Tanya's crosshairs. She spun around, then dashed toward the dock where, God willing, she would find another option—

Time careened to a stop as a gunshot blasted.

"Aaa-deee-laaide! I see you!" Tanya's voice was scarcely audible over the blustering wind, but nevertheless, her words sliced through Addie. Switching gears, and without wasting time to look for her pursuer, Addie pivoted away from the dock and made for the woods. She wobbled in the turn, almost falling again before picking up her stride.

Another crack and a bullet ripped through the air, striking the ground perilously close to Addie in an explosion of water and mud. Her feet pounded the ground with every ounce of strength she had left, praying she would reach the tree line before Tanya closed in on her.

Please let the rain keep Tanya from getting off a good shot.

Her prayers streamed in an endless plea as she blindly sped in the general direction Sam had indicated when pointing out the cottage. As she drew closer to the ominous woods, its trees swaying in the tempest, towering over her like violent giants about to strike, the path to the cottage materialized in the darkness. Not wanting to be easily followed, she turned from it and dashed down the line of trees. Finally, she made a hard right, veering into the woods on a trajectory she hoped was parallel to the cottage path.

She didn't dare look back to see if Tanya was following. She couldn't afford to slow down, though intertwining fatigue and fear made it feel like she had to keep reminding her legs to run.

She scrambled over brush and wound between trees, low branches slapping her in the face. The cuts stung sharply, but Addie was grateful for the jolt to her senses, which were growing duller by the second. Raw disgust churned in her gut at her self-destructive reaction to the danger. If shutting down continued to be her body's coping mechanism, it would doom her to whatever fate Tanya had planned. She clenched her fists.

Find the cottage.

She had to get her hands on another weapon—a knife or a shovel or *something*—and locate a landline, cellphone, or computer to contact the outside for help. Of course, if the Wi-Fi was off in the cottage as it was in the house, a computer wouldn't do her any good. Still, she had to try. If it came to nothing, she would hide in the tunnel until Sam or someone else showed up.

Thunder rolled over the sky as lightning flashed, illuminating her path briefly. Addie pushed her injured ankle to the limit, keeping a steady pace through the thicket, weaving between trees and hurdling over fallen limbs. She couldn't hear Tanya behind her, but she did not doubt she was still back there.

How had two people independently come up with schemes to kill someone and frame me for it? What are the chances? How unlucky can I be?

And can someone actually be that unlucky?

Maybe it wasn't chance at all. Maybe Richard and Tanya had been in on it together and Tanya had turned on him. Maybe—

She was standing still amid a grouping of prickly bushes, water running down her face, and her clothes sticking to her body.

When did I stop running?

Addie frantically glanced around for Tanya. She wasn't in sight, but that didn't mean she wasn't closing in. Fearful she had lost the small lead she had, Addie took off again.

I don't even know for certain if I'm going the right way. A wail threatened to erupt from her lungs.

Stop it. You can't lose it. This has to be the way. You know it is.

But, she challenged herself, *Sam said this is a large island, at least as the private ones go.*

After this much running, she could be anywhere by now. Was she any closer to the cottage at all?

Addie had her answer several steps later while making her way through a tight clump of evergreens. Spotting a light in the near distance, she raced toward it, bursting out of the woods into a wide clearing. Nestled at the back of it was a stone cottage, a single lamp burning to one side of its front door. The charming structure resembled something out of a fairy tale, with a sloping roof, a front portico, and a chimney on the far side. She ran to the door and yanked on the handle.

Locked.

She sped around to the back where she found another entrance, also locked. Fortunately, this one had glass panes in it.

Addie knew what she had to do, but it was a risk. The noise might alert Tanya to where she was, but she didn't have another option. Addie snatched up a large rock from the loose border around the landscaped bed and smashed it into the lower pane.

The glass shattered but wasn't quite as loud as Addie had anticipated. Muttering a prayer of thanks, she carefully reached through, nicking herself on a jagged shard in the process. Her fingers found a smooth, egg-shaped metal knob.

Yes!

She turned it, her heart lifting when it opened.

Addie slipped inside, careful to avoid the glass shards on the floor. She stood in a galley-type kitchen with an eating area off to one side. She would have propped a chair from the table under the doorknob in the hopes of keeping Tanya out, but after smashing the window, there was no point.

The lights had to stay off to avoid alerting Tanya to her whereabouts, but with the moonlight increasing now that the storm seemed to be waning, she was able to see well enough. She opened drawers, looking for knives and found a wood-handled set in the third one. After grabbing the knife she thought would be easiest to wield, Addie scanned the room.

No landline, phone or computer.

She rifled through the rest of the drawers, but came up empty. Moving on to the modest sitting room along the front of the house, Addie crept to a window to peer out at the clearing, keeping herself hidden behind the drapes.

There was no sign of Tanya.

But how long do I have before that changes?

Returning her attention to the room, Addie scoured the furniture and bookshelves for anything helpful, but again came up empty. She started charging up the stairs to the second level when the crack of a gunshot sounded. Her white-knuckled fingers curled around the banister for several moments before she came to herself.

Move, move, move!

Every nerve ending vibrating, her heart galloping, she sprinted back to the front window, spying out from behind the curtain again.

She was standing in the clearing, a specter draped in shadow, poised to attack.

Terror like waves bashing against one another reverberated through Addie, the force threatening to drop her to her knees. She whirled away from the window, pressing into the wall for support, trying to calm her runaway breath. The image of the killer standing in the clearing, holding the raised gun, burned in her mind.

"Aaa-deee-laaide!" came the taunting voice once again.

Shock coursed through Addie's every pore, her cells igniting and going numb all at once.

The killer had found her, and there was nowhere left to run.

34

ADDIE

She was trapped. As a voice in her head screamed at her to go, Addie considered her options, though her mind felt sluggish in the effort. Exhaustion and fear were taking their toll.

She couldn't go out the front. But the back?

How much farther does the island go? Are there enough woods behind the cottage to hide in?

She might go ten yards and find herself at the water. Then what?

If Addie went upstairs, and the killer came inside, Addie might be able to drop from one of the windows before she was found. Addie would have a decent head start and might be able to make it back to the tunnel before being spotted.

If her ankle survived the drop.

It wasn't a great plan, but it was the only one she had.

Clenching the banister like a lifeline, Addie pulled herself upward, favoring the ankle that ached intensely. The stairs ended at one end of a short hallway that ran along the backside of the cottage. Three closed doors spanned the wall on her left. Hoping to give herself as much time as possible before being found, Addie ran to the last one. As her hand landed on the doorknob, a faint squeak from downstairs met her ears.

Was it a door opening? A floorboard?

It didn't matter. Addie quietly opened the door enough to slide inside the gap, locking it behind her.

I need a chair, or a dresser or something to shove against it. So I'll have enough time to—

The rest of the thought evaporated as she wheeled around in her attempt to find something that would work and heard her own horrified scream pierce the air.

35

NOT ADDIE

A ddie's scream tore through the house, the terror that infused it almost palpable. A sardonic chuckle slithered out.
There it is.
Both feet hit the hallway at the top of the stairs and strode for the room at the end.
Now for the finale.

36

ADDIE

Addie slapped her hand against her mouth, extinguishing her scream.

Tanya lay on the bed, flat on her back, staring unseeing at the ceiling. A wide brown stain covered her shirt, with streaks bleeding down both sides.

No! No, no no....

Addie's heart seized as she ripped her gaze away, spinning in a circle looking for answers. For a plan. For a weapon.

For anything.

Her head swam. The adrenaline that should be clarifying her thoughts was muddying them beyond use. She moved to the side of an upholstered chair in the corner, intending to wedge it beneath the door handle. Setting the knife in the seat to free both hands, she grabbed the top of the chair's high back and dragged it. The chair wasn't very heavy, but at the right angle—

The Offer

The door burst open, slamming into Addie. The force ripped the chair from her hands and sent her flying back. She landed flat against the wall, her palms reaching back to steady herself as she looked directly into the face of the person who was going to end it all.

Addie's heart seized as she ripped her gaze away, spinning in a circle looking for answers. For a plan. For a weapon.

37

ADDIE

Time slowed. Addie oddly processed the scene as if in a trance, noticing things that didn't matter, because what did matter was too hard to digest.

Roses on the wallpaper. A gilded mirror on the wall to her left. No sound of rain. It must have stopped. Beams of moonlight broke through the sheers covering the single window, illuminating the room and the people in it.

Keeley Farrow looked so much like her father, Addie easily detected Richard's eyes, nose, and cheekbones in the young woman. She was perfectly recognizable from the photos in the family room, though she looked a few years older. Monica probably hadn't bothered to update them with current ones.

She probably hadn't bothered much with Keeley at all.

Addie blinked and attempted to back up despite already pressing against the wall. When she couldn't move any farther, she

The Offer

prayed.

Lord, save me. Please. But if not, bring me home to You. Forgive—

"What, you've got nothing to say?" Keeley said, gesturing at Addie with the gun. "After all this? I'm surprised." She brushed her hair back with one hand. Her strawberry-blond strands with their dark roots were a matted, dripping mess.

"I...I don't know what you want me to say!" Addie bellowed back, shaking, her mind working to process what was happening.

This woman had killed people.

She had killed Richard, and most likely Tanya.

Now she was here to kill Addie. Saying the wrong thing might be fatal. Saying nothing might be fatal too.

"I want you to ask," Keeley said.

Confusion reigned in Addie. She was so tired, and Keeley wasn't making sense. "Ask you what?"

"How? Why? All those questions." Keeley sighed, tilting her head and eyeing Tanya on the bed. "Yeah. I feel bad about her. She wasn't part of the plan. She wasn't supposed to be here but Monica forgot to cancel her, so I had to."

Disgust trickled down Addie's spine at Keeley's casual attitude toward her murder of the housekeeper. "You...had to? She was an innocent person who just happened to be here."

"Innocence doesn't come into it. You're innocent, and here you are. I did what I had to do, Addie. Here's the thing, though. I'll tell you why. Don't you want to know?"

Addie's lips buzzed with nervous energy as she considered the unhinged woman before her. Why didn't she just shoot her and get it over with? Why stand here and—

"You're wondering why you're not dead yet? Why I'm still talking to you?" Keeley asked, folding her arms across her chest with the gun at the front, ready to point if needed.

She was egging Addie on. Pressing her to ask. For some reason,

Keeley *wanted* to talk. If Addie's only hope was delay, then delay was what she needed to do. Delay and engender some empathy.

Addie nodded. "I am," she whispered. As she spoke the words, her legs did what they had been wanting to do for the last half hour and gave out. She slid down the wall until she sat on the floor, her knees at her chest.

A small smile erupted on Keeley's face, which lit up with anticipation. "Okay, so...I'm a scriptwriter...well, playwright, if I had my way. Did Monica tell you that?" The smile turned into a sharp frown. "I know my father wouldn't have. He wouldn't have mentioned me at all."

"Actually, she...she said you did a lot of things. I think she mentioned you wrote scripts."

"How far up was her nose turned when she said it?"

Addie didn't answer. She blinked, working to stay focused. To keep her composure.

I need to say the right thing.

"That's what I thought." Keeley sniffed. "Do your parents believe in you, Addie? Do they support you?"

"Yes," Addie answered softly.

"Must be nice. Dad—Richard—thought I was a waste of time and money. 'All that education, wasted,' he would say. He never seemed to remember I never *asked* to go to prep school. 'You're squandering it on your ridiculous artist garbage,'" she said in a spite-filled imitation of Richard's voice, then snorted. "Can you believe that? Here I am, trying to make something of myself, to use my passions to *be somebody* and make it on my own, and he calls it a waste." Her eyes narrowed. "Have your parents ever called you a waste, Addie?"

Addie shook her head. The room spun.

Keeley paced in front of the door. "It feels *great,*" she said, sarcasm dripping from her words. "You know what he told me two

The Offer

weeks ago?" She didn't wait for Addie to answer before continuing. "He wasn't going to give his hard-earned money to a mooching good-for-nothing who wasn't going to make anything useful of herself. Told me he was taking me out of his will when he met with his attorney next month and giving my share to their little elementary-school golden boy. What do you think about that?"

Addie sat quietly for a second. How could she respond without making things worse? "That's awful, Keeley."

"Yeah, well, I'm used to him being awful. But I wasn't prepared to have my share of his kingdom go to that money-grubbing wife of his and their spoiled spawn. Which brings me to the 'how' question." She raised her eyebrows. "Know what the worst thing is for a writer?"

Addie slowly shook her head.

"To never have anyone read your work. Or *watch* it, in my case. To spend all that time and effort—blood, sweat, and tears—and never have anyone experience it or know you created something brilliant. Imagine creating a three-star Michelin meal no one ever tasted. You can relate to that, right?"

"I can," Addie whispered.

"That's why I'm going to tell you. Because I *need* someone to know." Keeley sat down cross-legged on the floor, just feet from Addie, pointing the gun's muzzle at Addie's heart. "So, once upon a time..."

38

KEELEY
THREE WEEKS EARLIER

"Self-absorbed, useless old man," Keeley griped as she thrust all the clothing from her top drawer into a moving box. She repeated the process with the next drawer, also tossing out a few more colorful barbs about her father.

Heat still flushed her skin even though their argument had ended half an hour before. With anger pulsing like the backbeat to a heavy metal song, hard and violent, she yanked open the next drawer which held, not clothes, but her work. Scores of notebooks containing all her ideas for screenplays, stories, and stage plays she had written over the years from middle school through college. Her father would think they should go straight into the trash can. He would think they were a monument to her wasting her life on a "pointless, insane pastime that wasn't going to take her anywhere in life." He had screamed those exact words at her when she balked

The Offer

at his pronouncement that he was done supporting a mooching slug.

No more credit cards. No more condo in LA. No more anything. Either she could go to work for him and start making something of herself, or she could kiss the Richard Farrow money pipeline goodbye.

She would rather die than work for him. She wasn't like Justin, who loved all that computer stuff and was "making good on his own" as their father put it.

Well, good for Justin.

He had managed to get out and he had done it working at something their father respected, so he was still in Richard Farrow's good graces.

Her, not so much.

"Why can't you be more like your brother?" he had snapped from behind the massive oak desk in his home office.

"Because I'm an artist!" she had screamed back, slapping her palms on the desktop.

"You're a starving artist now. Because I'm done. And I'm taking you out of the will the next time I see my attorneys."

"No! Dad—"

"It's done," he said, his steely tone cutting her off and letting her know he wouldn't tolerate any further discussion. "Pack your things and straighten out your finances, because as of right now, you're getting nothing more from me. Boxes are waiting for you in your room. I want you gone by the time I get back tonight."

He stormed out after that, leaving her to burn in the fiery aftermath of the bombshell he had dropped. She grunted in disgust at the recollection, shoving the notebooks into a box. She plopped down on the bed, taking a long look around the room that had been hers since she was twelve—since before her mom passed, before step-monster number one, Emilia, and current step-monster,

Monica. It had started out pink, then been painted dark green in middle school, then black after her creative awakening in high school.

Well, partly because of that, and partly to tick off Monica.

She had left it that way ever since and was surprised Monica hadn't re-painted it. Especially since she was already in college once Monica came along. On second thought, that would have required Monica to be around Keeley's things, and both Monica and Richard Farrow preferred to pretend he didn't have a daughter.

What are you going to do? You've got no money, no real job, and no agent.

She would never admit it to her father, but the scriptwriting wasn't going well. Despite sending out project after project, no agent had taken the bait. All she had received was the standard rejection, *"Thank you for your submission. We regret it's not right for our agency at the moment..."*

She had never had her father's moral support, but at least she'd had his money. Now she wouldn't even have that. His money was what allowed her to write and kept her from having to work a job that would get in the way of her perfecting her craft and landing an agent.

Ire rose in her throat. How dare he cut her lifeline. How dare he take this cheap shot just to control her. It was so humiliating, him kicking her out like this, having the boxes waiting in her room as if she was an employee he had fired and now was making her clean out her desk.

He can't do this. Not without consequences. When I walk out of here, I'm not leaving empty-handed.

Springing off the bed, she abandoned her room and marched down the hall. Her father kept a stash of money in his office. She had pilfered from it when she was a teen, taking a hundred here and there. Nothing he would ever notice.

If it's still there, I'll be taking a lot more than a single hundred-dollar bill.

Her anger smoldered as she made her way through the Upper West Side brownstone until she was not only ready to steal from her father, but mercilessly ransack his precious office. Her insides warmed like a kid on Christmas at the thought of tossing his drawers, pouring his three-hundred-dollar-a-bottle scotch all over the floor, and incinerating a few of his first-edition Dickens novels.

She was so consumed with the notion that when she reached the second level, she didn't register Monica's voice until she was nearly at the woman's bedroom door. Monica had moved into a separate bedroom from Richard at some point after the beginning of the year—Keeley wasn't sure when and didn't care.

Monica's sharp tone carved into whoever was on the other end of the call. Keeley stalled her momentum, stopping right before Monica's door. She pressed her body flat against the hallway, listening hard. Given how loud Monica was speaking, she apparently didn't realize someone else was upstairs. It would be an easy mistake to make. Keeley had only been to the house twice since January, and when she arrived Monica had been at her early morning yoga class. She doubted her father told Monica she was there. She got the impression they hardly spoke.

"I'm telling you, this is my chance," she heard Monica say. "He's talking about making changes to his will and I can't just leave. I'll lose everything in the prenup. This is my chance. The perfect opportunity to get rid of him without sacrificing a thing." Silence filled the space briefly and Keeley forced herself to breathe as quietly as possible. "No, I've never seen her. But I've seen his phone. I know who she is and where she is. It'll be...no, listen. It'll be easy. You want to be together, Drake?" Another pause. "Then trust me."

Drake? The trophy wife has a boyfriend. No surprise.

The sound of footsteps falling on hardwoods invaded the hallway. Keeley guessed Monica was pacing as she spoke. "She's a chef, right?" Monica said. "So we use that. It's Richard's birthday soon. I'll plan a quiet getaway on the island. I'll hire Louis and make him so angry, he'll quit at the last minute. That'll be my cover. I'll go to her and tell her Richard's such a fan, he loves her food—which is true, by the way. He came home twice raving about this one dessert he loves after eating at her restaurant. I'll offer her an amount she can't refuse."

Time stretched until Monica spoke up again, her voice thick with exasperation. "What do you mean it'll never work? Of course it will. She's a new restaurateur in Manhattan. I'm sure she's drowning in debt. She'll come out and make his favorite, only before she serves it, I'll add a little something, and...no, I've already thought this through. The sweetness will cover up the bitter taste of the meds. I'll need your help with the dosage—"

Drake must have interrupted because she broke off in mid-sentence before excitedly starting in again. "Because I need to make sure the dosage kills him. I can't have him waking up afterward and I don't know how much of my depression meds it'll take to do that. You're the pharmacist...okay, pharmacy tech, whatever. Either way, figure it out so I do it right. She'll make the dessert he can't shut up about and I'll slip in the kitchen and mix the meds in it. He'll eat it and fall face first in his birthday dinner." A crude snicker escaped the room. "I'll tell the police I got lucky and didn't want any. I was full. 'I can't believe I was so close to dying, officer,'" she said, adopting a pitiful tone.

Monica went quiet briefly before piping up again. "Simple. Do you still have the gun you showed me?...Good. I'll use it. I'll say she pulled it on me when she realized I hadn't eaten any of the laced dessert. I'll say she was fuming, talking about wanting revenge on Richard and me for ruining her chances with him. I've been following him and I'm pretty sure they aren't seeing each other anymore, so that should square up with a story about her wanting to get him back or get revenge, whichever. I'll say we struggled for the gun and she got shot in the chaos. I'll shed some tears and make it look good. Before they come, I'll plant some of my meds in her room somewhere, so it looks like—"

She cut herself off, before squawking, "What do you mean why would she use *my* medication? If I'm going to say *she* was behind it, then her plan would have to be to make it look like I was the one who was trying to kill *her and Richard*. She would have to use something that would point the finger at me, so I have to use the same thing. That's why it's going to have to be my meds. I'll say Richard had told her about my depression and migraines—it'll be one of the reasons he left her, because he didn't feel right abandoning me with my issues. That will explain how she knew I'd have the medication with me. Better yet, I can say I caught her in my room, looking around."

Drake must have been talking a lot because Monica was mute for a couple of minutes. "No. When he dies, it takes care of everything. I won't have to divorce him to be rid of him and so the prenup means nothing. I'll end up with half, and the other half will go to his kids. We'll be set. You'll be moving in here before you know it, baby."

Keeley crept back to her room, doing her best not to make any noise. If Monica knew Keeley had heard her phone call, she wouldn't go through with it.

And Keeley needed her to go through with it.

Because Monica wasn't the only one who wanted Richard Farrow in the ground as soon as possible.

39

ADDIE

Addie's brain felt thick, her body heavy, and her heart faint. Even so, after Keeley's tale, one incredulous thought rang clearly through the fog.

Monica tried to kill me too. There are three murderers on this island, and I was the scapegoat for all of them.

"Obviously, things didn't go as Monica planned," Keeley said. "When I realized I had the perfect opportunity to not only get rid of my dad before he cut me out of his will, but also get rid of the gold-sucking leech, I jumped on it. No more splitting Dad's millions with the step-monster," Keeley said, a tiny smirk on her face like she was discussing a prank she cleverly pulled, not the murder of her father and attempted murder of her stepmother.

Keeley searched Addie's face in a way that suggested she was waiting for Addie to voice her awe at Keeley's grand plan. But Addie

The Offer

wasn't in awe. She was three seconds from vomiting. Keeley's eyebrows rose. "You're looking a little green."

"I'm fine." As soon as she said it, she reconsidered whether she should have. Maybe her only chance of escaping depended at least in part on Keeley believing Addie wasn't capable of putting up a fight. If Keely was a little too confident, Addie might catch her off guard. The only problem was, given the way she was feeling, Addie doubted that putting up a fight was a realistic option.

Keeley squinted. "You have to admit, the setup was perfect. I mean, Monica did all the legwork and none of it could be traced back to me. I basically only had to change one thing."

Keeley looked expectantly at Addie again. When Addie still didn't respond, Keeley groaned. "Come on, Addie. I had to take Monica out at the same time as Dad. I laced the salad dressing with a heavy-duty dose of her own meds, so there wouldn't be two different murder weapons. You know—one in the dessert, a different one in the salads? That would raise questions. This way it just looked like the killer—*you*, in the police's view—overdid it by dosing lots of the food to make sure Richard and Monica ended up dead. Monica had already set you up by lacing the desserts, so I let that ride. You'd have to hash it out with the cops, but in any event, they wouldn't be looking at me, because no one would know I'd ever been here."

Addie's eyes reflexively cut to Tanya, and Keeley followed them. "Yeah, except for her. I've been holed up in the cottage for a week getting ready for this—breaking their boat, setting up the cameras… It was easy enough to speed over on a jet ski, stash it on the other side of the island, and set up base in the cottage. They never come over here. Then Monica had to go and send *her* to clean it over the weekend. I mean, I get it. It was Monica's only option to get rid of her without raising questions. She needed Tanya out of the house. She couldn't have a witness around given what she was planning."

She clicked her tongue. "Monica was such an idiot. Forgetting to cancel the housekeeper?" Her eyes raked over Tanya's body again. "I didn't have a choice once she walked in on me. Her knowing I was on the island would have ruined everything. She ran up here too when I chased her, just like you. I guess it's because it's the last room on the hall? Farthest away? Anyway, I...dealt with it." She shrugged unconcernedly, sniffed, then continued. "I'll make it look like she caught you in the middle of doing something and you had to kill her to keep her quiet. It'll make sense, plot-wise."

"Tanya had nothing to do with this," Addie whispered, grief for the unsuspecting woman making her eyes sting with tears.

Keeley ignored her. "The rest of the story gets twisty. The best ones always do. Everything was set and you, Monica, and Dad were in your places," she said, blinking slowly before continuing as if scanning a script only she could see. "I was watching all of you from the wireless feed, just down the hall actually..."

A chill trickled down Addie's spine. *Wireless cameras?*

"...in case anything unexpected happened and I needed to make changes on the fly. And, wow, what Dad did was definitely unexpected. I have to give him credit. Somehow, he managed to plant the pills he was talking about without me seeing it on the video." She let out a chuckle devoid of humor, her eyes raking over Addie's features. "If you're banking on someone finding the cameras, don't. I'll collect them all long before the cops get here. Speaking of wireless, that's another thing. Dad changing the Wi-Fi password to keep you off the computer once you got away from him? Brilliant. He was a lot of things, but stupid wasn't one of them. Anyway, I saw him go into your room, but from that angle, I couldn't see exactly what he was doing. I thought he was just being his normal creepy self, going through your luggage. If I'd realized he was planting evidence, I might have seen it coming."

The Offer

Keeley chuckled again. "It's still hard to believe he came up with the same idea Monica and I did. I'm guessing he took one look at you and realized he could get rid of the overbearing, fortune-spending spouse, avoid the prenup—he had to pay if they divorced and she could prove he was cheating—and blame it on you. Abracadabra, no wife, no divorce payouts, and no jail. You can imagine my shock. There I was, watching my phone, waiting for the salad course to take them both out and BAM!" She slapped the floor. "Monica keels over before she touches it! I couldn't believe it. Then I heard Dad's whole speech and realized he beat me to it. Even used the same meds we did—but that's not surprising. Not many choices when you consider Monica's meds had to be the murder weapon to make any of our stories work and to trigger a heart attack. Luckily, she's got extra stashed everywhere. The woman was practically a pharmacy herself."

Keeley looked off into nowhere as if remembering something, and for a moment Addie considered trying to overpower her. Before she had a chance to do anything about it, Keeley's gaze settled back on her.

"At first, I panicked a little and had to improvise because there was no way Dad was going to eat anything from that table after Monica was dead, right? What would the cops think if they showed up and it looked like he had gone on with dinner with his wife—a corpse—on the floor and you locked upstairs? Since I couldn't overdose him, I had to switch to the gun. Monica had stashed it in one of the sideboard drawers—probably so she could take you out right away. I *had* planned on rushing in once they were both dead, grabbing it, and dealing with you. Instead, when he followed you upstairs, I took it, then hid until he came back down and, well, you know the rest."

Addie's stomach roiled, thinking of Richard in his study, red pooling around him. His daughter, shooting him in cold blood. Weakness flooded her. "He was your father."

Keeley's expression soured, her face stony. "He might have been the man who brought me into this world, but that was it. He never loved me. *Never*. Then he has the nerve to threaten to take away his money, the only thing he ever *did* give me? No. No way." She sniffed and shrugged her shoulders back, her expression becoming lighter. "So now you know. There it is. My script—with a few improvisations because of Dad. Some of my best work." An ironic snort escaped her. "Who would've thought he'd be a central character in one of my productions? Not him, that's for sure."

"They don't…the police…don't have to know. I won't—"

"No. Don't say you won't tell them, because we both know that isn't true. But I need you to understand that I didn't plan to do it this way. I'm not a monster. First, my dad ropes you into his sleazy web with his lies, and then Monica makes you part of this situation. I was going to let you live—though I'd still need to frame you. But, when you saw me walking outside in the middle of the night, things changed. I was pretty sure you wouldn't know it was me, but I couldn't take the chance you thought it was someone other than Monica. If you mentioned to the police that you saw someone outside when everyone was supposed to be inside, they might suspect another person had been on the island and start asking questions I didn't want asked. So I had to switch to Plan B."

Confusion clouded Addie's head again. *What is she talking about?*

After several seconds of misty bewilderment, the answer crystallized. Last night she had been looking out the window and saw what she thought was Monica walking near the water's edge. Only, it wasn't Monica. It must have been Keeley near the water. Near the kayaks.

That's what happened to them. Keeley hacked them up.

The Offer

Addie blinked, bringing her gaze to meet Keeley's. The woman's expression was blank, her lips pressed together. Keeley had apparently reached the end of her explanation. As the silence between them stretched, Addie grew more and more terrified. If Keeley was done talking, she had no reason to keep Addie alive any longer.

She needed to press Keeley to continue speaking, to keep explaining. "Don't have to...do this," Addie mumbled. "They'll...think—"

Keeley cocked her head. "It's really hitting you now, isn't it?"

Addie blinked some more. *What is she saying?* She tried to bring Keeley into focus, but her edges were growing blurry.

"I slipped a roofie in your tea," Addie barely heard Keeley say. "It was a risk. I couldn't have done it without the video feed to know where you all were when I snuck in the house. But I had to do something to incapacitate you. Otherwise, how was I going to stage your suicide? It's not like you would shoot yourself without a little help. I must not have given you enough, though. It took more time to kick in than I thought it would, but that stuff's not one-size-fits-all. Or so I'm told. Shouldn't be much longer now."

Addie's head rolled on her neck as she worked to register what Keeley was saying. All this time, she thought she'd been rendered dysfunctional by panic. She had been angry at herself for how paralyzed she had become in the face of danger. Now she knew it wasn't fear that had made her tired, clumsy, and fuzzy-headed. Whatever drug Keeley had slipped her was responsible for all of it.

Not that it matters now.

Addie's grip on herself loosened further and she slumped the rest of the way to the floor. She lay on her side, looking up at Keeley, unable to so much as lift her arms. Addie's insides free-fell, the strong sensation of tumbling down a bottomless pit overtaking her.

"I'm sorry it has to be this way," Keeley said, her voice faint now.

Addie's vision narrowed to a pinpoint of clarity, until she was hardly able to see Keeley as the woman leaned over her.

"Thanks for listening. I wanted someone to know. I know you'll keep my secret." She looked at the gun in her hand. "You'll keep all the secrets."

40

ADDIE

So this was how it ended. Slipping into unconsciousness, unable to protect herself. Unable to stop Keeley Farrow from killing her.

Addie's senses were failing her. Her vision was one big blur now. Streaks of white and gray against color, swirling together, making it impossible to detect where one shape ended and another began. The sound of Keeley's voice was an indistinct, muffled noise, the syllables of her words indistinguishable.

The only thing she was able to isolate was one thought cycling through her brain.

Keeley's going to kill me now. She's drugged me so I can't fight back. She'll make me pull the trigger.

From the mire of Addie's mind, an image surfaced of Keeley holding Addie's hand on the gun, then holding it to Addie's head, preparing to pull the—

No! Addie screamed, or tried to, but her mouth wouldn't move and her vocal cords wouldn't generate sound. Her panicked cry was only in her head as she willed Keeley away from her. But Keeley only drew closer—picking up Addie's hand...pressing it around the gun's grip.

Lord, if I'm done here, bring me home to you. Addie thought she might be crying, but couldn't feel her face anymore. She didn't want to leave yet. There was still so much she wanted to do, but it was out of her hands.

Addie's eyelids fell as, resignedly, she waited for the sound of the shot. An unexpected peace settled on her, the panic that had been strangling her releasing its grip. Her thoughts drifted to what her mind's eye would see in her last moment.

Would there be a brilliant flash? Or would a darkness deeper than she was in now momentarily descend on her?

What would be the first thing to meet her gaze when the curtain of death was pulled back and she stood in heaven's doorway?

She didn't find out, because the shot didn't come.

Instead, enraged shouting blasted the room and Addie's hand fell lifeless to the floor. Pain shot up from her legs as something crashed into them, then rolled off. Shock and confusion feebly reignited her like the last sparks of a sputtering fire. She strained to summon the energy to raise her eyelids as the frantic, desperate noises crescendoed. Finally, she managed a thin slit that revealed hazy shapes locked in a vicious struggle.

Then there was screaming.

A gunshot.

And Addie sank into oblivion.

41

ADDIE

"Addie?"

She was in school. She had forgotten her homework. The teacher was calling on her.

"Addie? Can you hear me?"

How had she forgotten it? Now she would fail. She couldn't fail...

"Addie? Can you hear me?"

Addie blinked.

She wasn't in school. She was lying down. A face hovered over her. But it wasn't her teacher. She squinted. She knew that face.

"Sam?" she whispered, her voice coming back to her sounding tired and weak.

"Hey, there," he said, smiling. "Welcome back."

She blinked several times in succession, bringing the room into focus. White walls. A double window, bright light streaming through the blinds. A monitor and an IV bag stand, with a line running into her arm. Sam sitting in a chair beside her bed.

A hospital.

A hospital meant she was safe.

"Keeley," she muttered. "Keeley Farrow. She—"

"It's okay," Sam said, placing a hand on her arm to squeeze it gently before pulling it back. "She's in custody. You're safe."

"She killed Monica...and Richard..."

Sam nodded. "They know. Or they're figuring it out. The police want to talk to you as soon as you're able. When the doc clears it." He held up the call button. "I buzzed to let them know you're awake. Somebody should be in here soon to check you out. How do you feel?"

How do I feel?

"Fuzzy. Exhausted. Like I took antihistamines and chased them with a sleeping pill. But no pain." She paused, shifting to turn toward him slightly. "What happened? Did she shoot me?"

"No. I got to her before she could. You're just woozy from being drugged. They've treated you, and done some scans and blood work...said you'll be tired mostly, but otherwise should be fine." He pointed at her foot. "Though, you've got a sprain there that might take a few weeks to heal. What do you remember?"

What do I remember?

Thinking felt like trying to lift free weights with her mind. "The last thing was me sliding down the wall. She...she was going to make it look like I'd shot myself. Then..." The memory of wrestling shadows surfaced. "Was that you? In the room?"

Sam nodded.

"How did you find me? And...where did you come from?"

"I was only there because Monica had asked me to come back last night to pick Tanya up. I was tied up with another customer's electrical dock issue and told her it would probably be after nine, but she was insistent. Paid me extra for the late trip. I finished early and came on, even though I couldn't reach anyone. Of course, now I know why."

Monica. Addie looked down at her fingers intertwined in her lap, the name conjuring images of the woman dead on the dining room floor. A calculation pushed its way to the forefront of her mind. *If Monica had gotten her way, Richard and I would've been dead by the time Sam showed up. He would've been a witness for Monica to play up to. Both he and Tanya would have been.* The image of Tanya in the cottage bedroom flickered in her mind and sadness surged through her.

"Tanya's dead too," she said, wiping her moist eyes.

"I know." Sam leaned forward, placing a reassuring hand on her arm again.

"It's so wrong. Three people are dead. And poor Tanya, she was just in the wrong place at the wrong time, just like me." Addie looked up at Sam. "She was going to kill me."

"I know. I heard her."

Heard her?

After a few seconds, she understood. *He thinks I mean Keeley.*

"No, not just Keeley. Monica too," she corrected.

"What?" he asked, his face scrunching. "Addie, I think you're confused. Keeley was the one—"

"No." She coughed and tried to sit up, but her body wasn't having it.

"Whoa," he said, rising to help her lie back. "You probably shouldn't try that yet."

She nodded, easing her head back onto the stiff pillow. "I'm not confused...Monica was the first one to try..." Her voice broke, the words catching in her dry throat. She tried again. "...and then, Richard locked me up. Then Keeley..."

Addie cut herself off, registering that her explanation came off like the ramblings of a very disoriented person. She would have to wait until she was more clear-headed to tell them. So they wouldn't think she was confused. Then she would be able to spell out the complicated details to the police and Sam in a way that made sense. They needed to believe her. They needed to understand.

"It's okay," he said. "You can tell them all about it when you're a little more awake. Your parents are on their way. The police got in touch with someone, um...a 'Gillian,' I think they said...from your restaurant this morning. She gave the police your parents' contact information and they called them."

This morning?

"What time is it?" she asked.

He smiled at her, and the same warmth that rippled through her on Friday when she met him did so again. "Eight. You've been out for almost twelve hours."

"Twelve hours?" She had been unconscious the entire time, with no memory of anything after Sam had shown up in the cottage.

"Between whatever she drugged you with and the meds they gave you here, you needed your rest."

"I guess so." She couldn't believe Sam was here, sitting with her, waiting for her to wake up. Then again, she couldn't believe he had made it to her in the cottage, showing up at exactly the right time. "Sam, I don't understand how you found me. How did you know to go to the cottage?"

"I saw you bolting down the side of the house, past the dock, when I got close. Seemed pretty odd given the storm, so I figured something was wrong. I docked fast and ran after you. When I came around the front, I saw Keeley fire a shot in your direction." He shrugged. "That's when I *knew* something was wrong. I chased after her all the way to the cottage, keeping my distance since I wasn't armed. I've got a gun on the boat, but I didn't know I'd need it when I stepped off. Once I got upstairs, I heard her talking to you. I had already called 9-1-1 but wasn't sure how long they would be. It made me nervous, waiting. I wanted to try to take her down but I couldn't see what was going on in the room and I was afraid she would shoot you if I startled her. When she started talking about you keeping secrets, I knew I'd run out of time, so I took a chance."

A rush of emotion flooded her at the thought of this stranger willing to risk his life for her. Again water gathered in the corners of her eyes. "You could've been shot."

He shrugged. "Couldn't let her shoot you. The timing, though...I admit that was pretty incredible. Someone was looking out for you," he said, squinting at the ceiling.

Addie felt a smile crack at the corner of her mouth. *Thank you, God, for that.*

Thank you.

Thank you.

"Seems like He was," she replied. Another intake of breath made her side ache and she shifted, trying to get comfortable. She must have done something to it in the fall—or when Sam and Keeley fell across her.

"You all right?" Sam asked, concern furrowing his brow.

"Yeah. I just...didn't stick the landing when I fell in that chute." She rubbed her hands over her face and sighed. "This story is crazy. I'm not sure they'll believe me."

Sam rubbed his chin. "They will. While I was hiding out in the hall, I managed to record most of Keeley's conversation with you."

"You did?"

"Yeah." He held out empty hands. "Which means I'm phone-less at the moment. They've got it in evidence. Who knows if I'll ever see it again."

"Sam, that's amazing."

"I don't know about 'amazing.'"

"Amazing. Incredible. Super-hero level. The comic-book guys have nothing on you," she said.

He laughed. "Sounds like maybe we need to decrease your pain meds a bit."

"I'm not on pain meds." *Am I?* She couldn't tell. "Am I?"

Sam grinned, snorting softly. "You're something else."

"You should see me when I'm not doped up." Maybe it *was* the pain meds, but she was feeling brave. "Come to my restaurant. In the city. I owe you. I'll make you the best dinner you've ever eaten. On the house."

His eyebrows rose. "On the house, huh?"

"One hundred percent."

"Don't know how I can turn that down," he said, the corner of his mouth shooting up.

"You can't."

"All right, Chef. It's a date. Now go to sleep."

Her heart fluttered. Maybe it was the pain meds.

Maybe not.

Either way, sleep sounded like a good idea.

42

ADDIE
THREE WEEKS LATER

"Two more specials," Addie called out to her sous chef over the din in the kitchen. Three people adorned in white aprons seared, sautéed, and stirred in the space, working in what might appear to be organized chaos. But it wasn't chaos. It was a well-oiled machine. The room was humming with the energy of a kitchen working hard to serve a packed dining room.

In the three weeks since the Thousand Islands nightmare, Addie had given multiple statements to the local police. Keeley's lawyers had worked out a deal for her, which meant Addie wouldn't have to relive it all by testifying in court, for which she was supremely grateful. Her ankle was healing, though she still wore a brace. It made the long nights of standing in the kitchen harder than before, though it wasn't anything she couldn't handle.

Gratitude was a covering over her days since coming back to

Manhattan. Gratitude that God heard her pleas and intervened to save her. Gratitude for a second chance. Gratitude for every moment she was breathing and the reminder that, though having a goal was admirable, an obsession with success was not. She had pushed too many things into the "later column" to focus solely on the restaurant. The single-minded purpose track was no way to live. Not to the exclusion of everyone and everything else that mattered. So, she had started back with her Saturday brunches with friends, scheduled her after-school readings with the neighborhood school, and stepped into church for the first time in quite a while.

It felt really good.

"How's that ankle holding up, Chef?" Gillian stood in the doorway of the office at the back of the kitchen, her eyebrows raised.

"Fine, mom," Addie replied, a smile curving her lips as she continued to work.

"Promise you'll say something if it gets to be too much?"

"I promise."

"Chef?" Derek, one of the waiters, called out.

Addie didn't look up from the olive oil she was pouring into a pan. "Yes?"

"One of the customers wants to speak with you."

Addie usually enjoyed engaging with customers, but tonight was the busiest they had ever been. One unexpected side effect of the news coverage of the "Spirits Island Slaughter," as the media was calling it, was people flocking to East to West. The last thing she needed to do was to leave the kitchen right now.

"Will you see if they can wait a bit? I'm slammed at the moment." She swirled the olive oil in the pan, then set it back on the gas burner.

"Um...I don't think you're gonna want to wait on this one, Chef."

That made Addie look up.

The Offer

So, another critic is visiting the restaurant.

She wasn't surprised. When a review was published like the stellar one Jonas Carter released last week, other critics followed soon after, either to confirm or challenge the review.

"Which table?"

"Fourteen," Derek answered.

Addie wiped her hands on her apron and turned away from the stove. "Cara, can you take over here?"

"Yes, Chef," answered the woman one station over. She stepped in to replace Addie, who headed for the swinging door leading into the dining room. She pushed through into the short hallway separating the two areas, the sounds of the kitchen fading as the low murmur of diners' voices backed by the tones of soft jazz rose in her ears. After a few strides, she turned the corner and stopped in place.

Sitting at table fourteen, with a wry grin on his face, was Sam.

"What are you doing here?" she asked, a smile drawing up her cheeks as she lowered into the chair across from him. "I thought you were getting in tomorrow?"

Sam shrugged. "Got here early. I have a habit of doing that," he said cheekily, and she knew they were both thinking of how she was only alive because he had arrived on the island before he was supposed to.

"No complaints about your timing here," she said, Sam chuckling as she continued, "but I can't leave until midnight at the earliest. Eleven thirty if I push it."

Sam leaned back. "I can kill a couple of hours. It's the city that never sleeps, right?"

"That's what they tell me." Addie scanned the table. There were no plates, only a few spots on the tablecloth. "You've already had dinner? I had no idea you were out here. I could have made you something special."

"Dinner was perfect. I promise to leave a great Yelp review."

"You better," she said, cocking her head and drawing her eyebrows up in mock admonition. He chuckled again, and she leaned forward. "Did you have dessert? Let me at least bring you that."

"No need," he said, reaching down to retrieve a light-blue box with a twine bow. He slid it across the table. "I brought you something."

She grinned. "You know it's bad form to bring food from one restaurant into another."

He pointed at the box, circling his forefinger. "Go on. I think you'll forgive me."

Addie pulled on the bow's ends, removed the undone twine, and opened the lid. Inside sat an enormous, perfectly golden, thickly-glazed cinnamon roll.

She laughed. "You certainly know the way to a woman's heart."

"I hope so," Sam retorted, flashing the grin she had first seen on her water taxi ride to Spirits Island. "I really hope so."

ACKNOWLEDGMENTS

Thank you to —

My readers, for spending your valuable time in my stories and spreading the word. You make this possible;

My wonderful beta readers: Laura Stratton, Gene Gettler, Tessa Hobbs, and Kimberly Pugh;

My secret weapon, Shaw Gookin, for his fact-checking genius and priceless story insights;

My medical guru, Dr. Michael Edwards, for his indispensable expertise;

My editors, Lesley McDaniel and Kim Kemery;

My friend, fellow author, and mentor, Luana Ehrlich;

My parents, Lynn and Bob Plummer, who have always encouraged my dreams; and,

My husband, Ron, for everything.

NOTE TO READERS

I hope you enjoyed *The Offer*, the second stand-alone book in the Deadly Decisions Collection. If you did, please tell your friends and leave a rating and review on Amazon, Goodreads, Bookbub, and whatever other social media platforms you enjoy. Reviews and word of mouth are what keep a novelist's work alive, and I would be extremely grateful for yours.

Would you like a free, award-winning short story?

Visit my website at www.dlwoodonline.com to learn about my books and subscribe to my newsletter, which will keep you updated (usually only twice a month) on free and discounted goodies, new releases, advance review team opportunities and more.

ABOUT D.L. WOOD

D.L. Wood is a *USA TODAY* bestselling author, Daphne du Maurier Award finalist, and two-time Illumination Book Awards Gold Medal winner. She writes thrilling suspense laced with romance and faith. In her novels she tries to give readers the same thing she wants: a "can't-put-it-down-stay-up-till-3am" character-driven story, full of heart, believability, and adrenaline. Her award-winning books offer clean, captivating fiction that entertains and uplifts.

D.L. lives in North Alabama, where, if she isn't writing, you'll probably catch her curled up with a cup of Earl Grey and her Westies—Frodo and Dobby—bingeing on the latest BBC detective series. If you have one to recommend, please email her immediately, because she's nearly exhausted the ones she knows about. She loves to hear from readers, and you can reach her at dlwood@dlwoodonline.com.

FOLLOW AUTHOR D.L. WOOD

It's a tremendous help to authors when readers follow us on social media. Don't miss a thing —follow me on these platforms so you'll know about my latest releases, bargains and more. Thank you!

Facebook
facebook.com/dlwoodonline
Instagram
instagram.com/authordlwood
Goodreads
goodreads.com/dlwood
Bookbub
bookbub.com/authors/d-l-wood
Twitter
twitter.com/dlwoodonline
Amazon
amazon.com/D.L.-Wood/e/B0165NBAMC
YouTube
bit.ly/AuthorDLWoodYouTube

SECRETS AND LIES ARE DANGEROUS THINGS

Boston police detective Dani Lake dreads returning to her hometown of Skye, Alabama, for her 10-year high school reunion. But not for the normal reasons.

At fifteen, Dani discovered the body of her classmate, and her failure to provide evidence leading to the killer resulted in the unjust conviction of her dear friend and a guilt burden she carried for life. When new evidence is unearthed during her visit, suggesting the truth she's always suspected, she embarks on a mission to expose the killer, aided by police detective Chris Newton, who just happens to be the man Dani's best friend is dying to set her up with, and the only person who believes her.

But when Dani pushes too hard, someone pushes back, endangering Dani and those closest to her as she uncovers secrets deeper and darker than she ever expected to learn—secrets that may bring the truth to light, if they don't get her killed first.

SECRETS SHE KNEW is the first of the stand-alone *Secrets and Lies Suspense Novels*.

GET YOUR COPY AND START READING NOW

BONUS EXCERPT FROM
UNINTENDED TARGET

Have you read D.L. Wood's *Unintended Series?* On the following pages is an excerpt from **UNINTENDED TARGET**, the first novel in this series which has captivated readers, with millions of pages read on Kindle Unlimited alone and an Illumination Awards Gold Medal for Best Christian Fiction ebook.

This series follows Chloe McConnaughey, an unsuspecting travel photojournalist, thrust into harrowing and mysterious circumstances ripe with murder, mayhem, and more. And by more, I mean a handsome man or two that seem too good to be true—and just might be. Turn to the next page to get started.

Amazon Reviews for UNINTENDED TARGET

"D.L. Wood truly does know how to captivate her readers; a master storyteller."

"Just the right balance of intrigue and a touch of romance."

"All I can say is buckle up, it's gonna be intense."

"Best book I have read in a while."

"It has been a long time since I stayed up until 3 am to finish a book in one sitting!"

"This book had all the components of an engrossing read…mystery, romance and best of all, great writing."

Goodreads Reviews for UNINTENDED TARGET

"…[A] story on steroids as it never let up with more twists and turns than I can remember."

"You can't find a book with more fast paced suspense than this one."

"I highly recommend not reading this book before bed, you'll not want to put it down."

"…twists and turns to entertain even the most demanding reader."

CHAPTER ONE

"He's done it again," groaned Chloe McConnaughey, her cell held to her ear by her shoulder as she pulled one final pair of shorts out of her dresser. "Tate knew that I had to leave by 3:30 at the latest. I sent him a text. I know he got it," she said, crossing her bedroom to the duffel bag sitting on her four-poster bed and tossing in the shorts.

Her best friend's voice rang sympathetically out of the phone. "There's another flight out tomorrow," offered Izzie Morales hesitantly.

Chloe zipped up the bag. "I know," she said sadly. "But, that isn't the point. As usual, it's all about Tate. It doesn't matter to him that I'm supposed to be landing on St. Gideon in six hours. What does an assignment in the Caribbean matter when your estranged brother decides it's time to finally get together?"

"Estranged is a bit of a stretch, don't you think?" Izzie asked.

"It's been three months. No texts. No calls. Nothing," Chloe replied, turning to sit on the bed.

"You know Tate. He gets like this. He doesn't mean anything by it. He just got ... distracted," Izzie offered.

"For three months?"

Izzie changed gears. "Well, it's only 3:00—maybe he'll show."

"And we'll have, what, like thirty minutes before I have to go?" Chloe grunted in frustration. "What's the point?"

"Come on," Izzie said, "The point is, maybe this gets repaired."

Chloe sighed. "I know. I know," she said resignedly. "That's why I'm waiting it out." She paused. "He said he had news he didn't want to share over the phone. Seriously, what kind of news can't you share over the phone?"

"Maybe it's so good that he just has to tell you in person," Izzie suggested hopefully.

"Or maybe it's—'I've been fired again, and I need a place to crash.'"

"Think positively," Izzie encouraged, and Chloe heard a faint tap-tapping in the receiver. She pictured her friend on the other side of Atlanta, drumming a perfectly manicured, red-tipped finger on a nearby surface, her long, pitch-colored hair hanging in straight, silky swaths on either side of her face.

"He'll probably pull up any minute, dying to see you," Izzie urged. "And if he's late, you can reschedule your flight for tomorrow. Perk of having your boss as your best friend. I'll authorize the magazine to pay for the ticket change. Unavoidable family emergency, right?"

Chloe sighed again, picked up the duffel bag and started down the hall of her two-bedroom rental. "I just wish it wasn't this hard." The distance between them hadn't been her choice and she hated it. "Ten to one he calls to say he's had a change of plans, too busy with work, can't make it."

"He won't," replied Izzie.

With a thud, Chloe dropped the bag onto the kitchen floor by the door to the garage, trading it for half a glass of merlot perched on the counter. She took a small sip. "Don't underestimate him. His over-achievement extends to every part of his life, including his ability to disappoint."

"Ouch." Izzie paused. "You know, Chlo, it's just the job."

"I have a job. And somehow I manage to answer my calls."

"But your schedule's a little more your own, right? Pressure-wise I think he's got a little bit more to worry about."

Chloe rolled her eyes. "Nice try. But he manages tech security at an investment firm, not the White House. It's the same thing every time. He's totally consumed."

"Well, speaking as your editor, being a *little* consumed by your job is not always a bad thing."

"Ha-ha."

"What's important is that he's trying to reconnect now."

Chloe brushed at a dust bunny clinging to her white tee shirt, flicking it to the floor. "What if he really has lost this job? It took him two years after the lawsuit to find this one."

"Look, maybe it's a promotion. Maybe he got a bonus, and he's finally setting you up. Hey, maybe he's already bought you that mansion in Ansley Park..."

"I don't *need* him to set me up—I'm not eight years old anymore. I'm fine now. I wish he'd just drop the 'big-brother-takes-care-of-wounded-little-sister' thing. He's the wounded one."

"You know, if you don't lighten up a bit, it may be another three months before he comes back to see you."

"One more day and he wouldn't have caught me at all."

Izzie groaned jealously. "It's not fair that you get to go and I have to stay. It's supposed to be thirty-nine and rainy in Atlanta for, like, the next month."

"So come along."

"If only. You know I can't. Zach's got his school play next weekend. And Dan would kill me if I left him with Anna for more than a couple days right now." A squeal sounded on Izzie's end. "Uggggh. I think Anna just bit Zach again. I've gotta go. Don't forget to call me tomorrow and let me know how it went with big brother."

"Bigger by just three minutes," she quickly pointed out. "And I'll try to text you between massages in the beach-side cabana."

Izzie groaned again, drowning out another squeal in the background. "You're sick."

"It's a gift," Chloe retorted impishly before hanging up.

Chloe stared down at the duffel and, next to it, the special backpack holding her photography equipment. She double-checked the *Terra Traveler* I.D. tags on both and found all her information still legible and secure. "Now what?" she muttered.

Her stomach rumbled, reminding her that, with all the packing and preparation for leaving the house for two weeks, she had forgotten to eat. Rummaging through the fridge, she found a two-day old container of Chinese take-out. Tate absolutely hated Chinese food. She loved it. Her mouth curved at the edges as she shut the refrigerator door. *And that's the least of our differences.*

Leaning against the counter, she cracked open the container and used her chopsticks to pluck julienne carrots out of her sweet and sour chicken. *Too bad Jonah's not here,* she thought, dropping the orange slivers distastefully into the sink. *Crazy dog eats anything. Would've scarfed them down in half a second.* But the golden retriever that was her only roommate was bunking at the kennel now. She missed him already. She felt bad about leaving him for two whole weeks. Usually her trips as a travel journalist for *Terra Traveler* were much shorter, but she'd tacked on some vacation time to this one in order to do some work on her personal book project. She wished she had someone she could leave him with, but Izzie was her only close friend, and she had her hands full with her kids.

Jonah would definitely be easier than those two, she thought with a smile. He definitely had been the easiest and most dependable roommate she'd ever had—and the only male that had never let her down. A loyal friend through a bad patch of three lousy boyfriends. The last of them consumed twelve months of her life before taking her "ring-shopping," only to announce the next day that he was leaving her for his ex. It had taken six months, dozens of amateur therapy sessions with Izzie and exceeding the limit on her VISA more than once to get over that one. After that she'd sworn off men for the foreseeable future, except for Jonah of course, which, actually, he seemed quite pleased about.

She shoveled in the last few bites of fried rice, then tossed the box into the trash. *Come to think of it,* she considered as she headed for the living room, *Tate'll be the first man to step inside this house in almost a year.* She wasn't sure whether that was empowering or pathetic.

"Not going there," she told herself, forcing her train of thought instead to the sunny beaches of St. Gideon. The all-expenses paid jaunts were the only real perks of her job as a staff journalist with *Terra Traveler,* an online travel magazine based out of Atlanta. They were also the only reason she'd stayed on for the last four years despite her abysmal pay. Photography, her real passion, had never even paid the grocery bill, much less the rent. Often times the trips offered some truly unique spots to shoot in. Odd little places like the "World's Largest Tree House," tucked away in the Smoky Mountains, or the home of the largest outdoor collection of ice sculptures in a tiny town in Iceland. And sometimes she caught a real gem, like this trip to the Caribbean. Sun, sand, and separation from everything stressful. For two whole weeks.

The thought of being stress-free reminded her that at this

particular moment, she wasn't. Frustration flared as she thought of Tate's text just an hour before:

Flying in tonite. Ur place @ 2. Big news. See u then.

Typical Tate. No advance warning. No, *"I'm sorry I haven't returned a single call in three months"* or *"Surprise, I haven't fallen off the face of the earth. Wanna get together?"* Just a demand.

A familiar knot of resentment tightened in her chest as she took her wine into the living room, turned up Adele on the stereo and plopped onto a slipcovered couch facing the fire. Several dog-eared books were stacked near the armrest, and she pushed them aside to make room as she sank into the loosely stuffed cushions. She drew her favorite quilt around her, a mismatched pink and beige patchwork that melded perfectly with the hodgepodge of antique and shabby chic furnishings that filled the room.

What do you say to a brother who by all appearances has intentionally ignored you for months? It's one thing for two friends to become engrossed in their own lives and lose track of each other for a while. It's something else altogether when your twin brother doesn't return your calls. He hadn't been ill, although that had been her first thought. After the first few weeks she got a text from him saying, *sorry, so busy, talk to u ltr.* So she had called his office just to make sure he was still going in. He was. He didn't take her call that day either.

She tried to remember how many times she'd heard "big news" from Tate before, but quickly realized she'd lost count years ago. A pang of pity slipped in beside the frustration, wearing away at its edges.

She set her goblet down on the end table beside a framed picture of Tate. In many respects it might as well have been a mirror. They shared the same large amber eyes and tawny hair, though she let her loose curls grow to just below her narrow shoulders. Their oval faces and fair skin could've been photocopied they were so similar. But he was taller and stockier, significantly out-sizing her petite, five foot four frame. She ran a finger along the faint, half-inch scar just below her chin that also differentiated them. He'd given her that in a particularly fierce game of keep-away when they were six. Later, disappointed that she had an identifying mark he didn't, he had unsuccessfully tried duplicating the scar by giving himself a nasty paper cut. In her teenage years she'd detested the thin, raised line, but now she rubbed it fondly, feeling that in some small, strange way it linked her to him.

He had broken her heart more than a little, the way he'd shut her out since taking the position at Inverse Financial nearly a year ago. He'd always been the type to throw himself completely into what he was doing, but this time he'd taken his devotion to a new high, allowing it to alienate everyone and everything in his life.

It hadn't always been that way. At least not with her. They'd grown up close, always each other's best friend and champion. Each other's only champion, really. It was how they survived the day after their eighth birthday when their father, a small-time attorney, ran off to North Carolina with the office copy lady. That was when Tate had snuck into their mother's bedroom, found a half-used box of Kleenex and brought it to Chloe as she hid behind the winter clothes in her closet. *I'll always take care of you, Chlo. Don't cry. I'm big enough to take care of both of us.* He'd said it with so much conviction that she'd believed him.

Together they'd gotten through the day nine months after that when the divorce settlement forced them out of their two-story Colonial into an orange rancher in the projects. Together they weathered their mother's alcoholism that didn't make her mean, just tragic, and finally, just dead, forcing them into foster homes.

And though they didn't find any love there, they did manage to stay together for the year and a half till they turned eighteen.

Then he went to Georgia Tech on a scholarship and she, still at a loss for what she wanted to do in life, took odd jobs in the city. The teeny one bedroom apartment they shared seemed like their very own castle. After a couple of years, he convinced her she was going nowhere without a degree, so she started at the University of Georgia. For the first time they were separated. But Athens was only a couple hours away and he visited when he could and still paid for everything financial aid didn't. She'd tried to convince him she could make it on her own, but he never listened, still determined to be the provider their father had never been.

When she graduated, she moved back to Atlanta with her journalism degree under her belt and started out as a copy editor for a local events magazine. Tate got his masters in computer engineering at the same time and snagged a highly competitive job as a software designer for an up-and-coming software development company. It didn't take long for them to recognize Tate's brilliance at anything with code, and the promotions seemed to come one after the other.

Things had been so good then. They were both happy, both making money, though she was only making a little and he, more and more as time went by. The photo in her hands had been taken back then, when the world was his for the taking. Before it all fell apart for him with that one twist of fate that had ruined everything—

Stop, she told herself, shaking off the unpleasant memory. The whole episode had nearly killed Tate, and she didn't like to dwell on it. It had left him practically suicidal until, finally, this Inverse job came along. When it did, she thought that everything would get better, that things would just go back to normal. But they didn't. Instead Tate had just slowly disappeared from her life, consumed by making his career work...

She brushed his frozen smile with her fingers. Affection and pity and a need for the only person who had ever made her feel like she was a part of something special swelled, finally beating out the aggravation she had been indulging. As she set the frame back on the table, her phone rang.

Speak of the devil, she thought, smiling as she reached for her cell.

"Hello?"

A deep, tentative voice that did not belong to her brother answered.

* * * * *

It never ceased to amaze him how death could be so close to a person without them sensing it at all. Four hours had passed and she hadn't noticed a thing. It was dark now, and rain that was turning to sleet ticked steadily on the car, draping him in a curtain of sound as he watched her vague grey shadow float back and forth against the glow of her drawn Roman blinds. He was invisible here, hunkered down across the street behind the tinted windows of his dark Chevy Impala, swathed in the added darkness of the thick oaks lining the neighbor's yard.

Invisible eyes watching. Waiting.

Watch. Wait. Simple enough instructions. But more were coming. Out of habit he felt the Glock cradled in his jacket and fleetingly wondered *why* he was watching her, before quickly realizing he didn't care. He wasn't paid to wonder.

He was just a hired gun. A temporary fix until the big guns arrived. But, even so...

He scanned the yard. The dog was gone. She was completely alone. *It would be, oh, so easy.*

But he was being paid to watch. Nothing more.

Her shadow danced incessantly from one end of the room to the other. Apparently the news had her pacing.

What would she do if she knew she was one phone call away from never making a shadow dance again?

THE STORY CONTINUES IN
UNINTENDED TARGET

GET YOUR COPY AND START READING NOW

BOOKS BY D.L. WOOD

THE UNINTENDED SERIES
Unintended Target
Unintended Witness
Unintended Detour

THE CRIMINAL COLLECTION
A Criminal Game

THE SECRETS AND LIES SUSPENSE NOVELS
Secrets She Knew
Liar Like Her

THE DEADLY DECISIONS COLLECTION
The Vow
The Offer
The Choice (Coming Soon)